A novel based on
the major motion picture

A novel based on the major motion picture

Screenplay by Robert Rodriguez
Adapted by Megan Stine

talk miramax books

HYPERION BOOKS FOR CHILDREN

NEW YORK

CREATED AND PRODUCED BY PARACHUTE PUBLISHING, L.L.C.

All photographs by Rico Torres.

First Edition
1 3 5 7 9 10 8 6 4 2

ISBN: 0-7868-1627-9

Library of Congress Catalog Card Number: 00-112159

SPY kids™

CHAPTER ONE

"**H**elp! I'm going to fall!" Juni Cortez cried.

His older sister, Carmen, glanced over. Juni was hanging from the high parallel bars in their family's workout room. So was she. "Don't let go, Butter-fingers!" Carmen teased.

Juni looked down. The floor was a zillion feet below.

His fingers started to slip.

Here we go, again, Juni thought miserably. My hands can never hold on tight enough.

Juni's hands were always a mess. Whenever he was nervous, warts popped out all over them. He had to use special medicine and wear lots of band-ages to hide the ugly bumps.

"Scaredy-cat," Carmen called. Then she swung her legs out and kicked her brother. Not too hard. Just enough to make him lose his grip.

"Ahhh!" Juni screamed as he hurtled through

the air. The floor seemed miles below him.

Carmen wasn't worried. She knew there was a net stretched below to catch him. Besides, their dad was standing nearby. He'll be fine, she thought, as she watched her brother fall.

Carmen flipped off the high bar and landed in the net beside Juni.

"You just fell a thousand feet!" Carmen teased. "You're a pancake."

"Am not," Juni argued, struggling to his feet.

"Are too," Carmen said. "Pancake man."

"Don't call me names," Juni shouted.

Carmen's dad came up and put a stern hand on her shoulder. "You're ten years old, Carmen. He's only eight. You're supposed to help *push* him," he reminded his daughter.

"But I did push him!" Carmen insisted. "Didn't you see?"

"Not like that." Her dad shook his head. "You know what I mean, Carmen. Push Juni as in *challenge* him. Not kick him off the bars!"

Carmen shrugged. "Sorry. Can I go eat breakfast now?"

Mr. Cortez sighed and nodded.

"Butterfingers," Carmen whispered to Juni as she passed him on her way toward the door. She wiggled her fingers at him.

Juni lunged for her, ready to fight. But his dad caught him by the arm and spun him around. Juni threw up his arms in a karate pose.

"Don't let Carmen get to you," Mr. Cortez said, ruffling his son's curly red hair. "You have to rise to her challenge. Match wits with her."

Match wits? Nah. Too hard, Juni thought. It was easier to beat his sister with a karate chop. Sometimes.

He whirled around and swung his arms at his dad. But Mr. Cortez was ready. He took the hit on his arm and stood in position, ready for more.

"Good, Juni!" his dad said. "That's exactly what I mean. Be ready for anything. Then maybe you won't get picked on so much at school."

"But I don't get picked on," Juni protested. "Not much anyway." He didn't want his dad to know how much the other kids teased him.

To prove how tough he was, Juni flew into another karate move. His dad stopped the blows every time.

Suddenly, Mr. Cortez looked closely at Juni's hands and frowned.

"You know, Juni, those warts come out because you're afraid," he said.

"No, they don't!" Juni said. "My hands just sweat a lot."

His dad bent down and put an arm around his son. "Imagine this," he said gently. "You're standing in front of a door. Behind the door is everything you fear. *Everything*! You don't want to open it—but you have to, Juni. You have to open that door—and face your fear. Only then can you overcome it."

"So where is the door?" Juni asked.

His dad rapped his knuckles on Juni's head. "The door is in here."

In my *head*? Juni thought. Weird!

"Come on, son," Mr. Cortez said. "Let's get some breakfast. Your mom and I have something important to tell you kids."

In the kitchen, Mrs. Cortez was making smiley-face pancakes. Sort of. She put two fried eggs in each pancake for the eyes. A piece of bacon was supposed to be the smiling mouth. But this morning, the bacon mouths were frowning.

"Mom, are you feeling okay?" Carmen asked.

"Oh. Sorry," her mother said. She turned the bacon mouths into smiles. "I'm just a little worried about something. Your . . . uh . . . your aunt is sick."

"We have an aunt?" Juni and Carmen glanced at each other in surprise. Their eyes opened wide.

"Well, yes," Mrs. Cortez said. "Your aunt . . . uh . . . "

"Gradenko," their father chimed in.

"Yes. Poor Aunt Gradenko. She's very sick," Mrs. Cortez said, nodding.

"So your mom and I have to go away for a few days," Mr. Cortez added.

"Cool! Can we come? We get to miss school!" Carmen cried.

"No way," her father said firmly. "You and Juni are staying here."

"Alone?" Carmen's eyes lit up hopefully.

Her dad shook his head. "Uncle Felix is coming to stay with you."

"Really? When?" asked Juni.

At that moment, the kitchen door banged open, and there stood Uncle Felix, his arms full of grocery bags.

"Uncle Felix!" Carmen and Juni cried. They both raced to give him a hug.

"Hey, kiddos," Uncle Felix said. He set down the groceries. "Last time I saw you kids, you were *this* tall!" He held his hand up high above their heads, as a joke. "You're shrinking!"

Juni and Carmen laughed. They loved their uncle Felix. He was always way more fun than Mom and Dad.

"Can we stay up late watching movies and eating caramel popcorn?" Juni asked.

Felix motioned toward the groceries. "Check the bag," he said.

Juni looked inside. Sure enough, there were two boxes of caramel corn right on top. "Bingo," Juni said. He pulled the popcorn out with a huge smile.

"Felix, why don't you take the kids and go get settled in?" Mrs. Cortez said. "Gregorio and I have to get ready to leave."

"Okay." Felix nodded. "Come on, kids."

As soon as they were out of earshot, Mrs. Cortez looked at her husband. "You know, Gregorio, one of these days, we'll have to tell the children the truth," she said.

"The truth?" Mr. Cortez repeated. "You mean . . . where we're going and what we're going to do?"

Mrs. Cortez nodded. "Yes. We've kept the secret too long. Sooner or later they're going to find out."

CHAPTER TWO

"**D**o you think the kids suspect already?" Mr. Cortez asked his wife as they hurried to their bedroom to pack. He flipped a switch on his desk, and a hidden computer keyboard popped up.

"No," Mrs. Cortez answered. "I don't. Even though I've told them a hundred times."

She pushed a few buttons on her dressing table. Immediately, her makeup mirror transformed into an electronic map of the world.

Mr. Cortez looked puzzled. "What do you mean? I thought we were keeping this a secret."

"The bedtime story," Mrs. Cortez explained. "Every night I tell them the truth about us—but they don't realize it. I tell them about the two international spies who were on opposite sides of danger. She was beautiful, and he was handsome—and they were both masters of disguise."

"Of course we were!" Mr. Cortez beamed.

"They could sense danger a mile away," Mrs. Cortez went on. "And through their work, wars were stopped before they even started."

"Those were the good old days," Mr. Cortez said, nodding. "He was the greatest spy his nation ever had."

"True," Mrs. Cortez said. "And she was the greatest spy *her* nation ever had—don't forget that! But remember, it was her mission to eliminate him."

"Krckkh!" Mr. Cortez said, making a terrible sound as he drew his finger across his neck. "And *his* mission was to eliminate *her*. Permanently," he added to the story.

"But instead of killing each other, they fell in love." Mrs. Cortez smiled at her husband.

"Of course they did." Mr. Cortez smiled back. "And that's when they quit the spy business to undertake the most dangerous mission of all. Getting married."

Mrs. Cortez sighed. "Then we had two children and became espionage consultants, working at home."

"Exactly," Mr. Cortez said. "And we've been happy ever since, haven't we?"

"Definitely," Mrs. Cortez answered, checking her reflection in the mirror. She had changed into slim black pants and a dark red top. She added a tight black jacket with the collar turned up. Then she put on her dark spy glasses. "I don't miss the old excitement at all. The action. The danger. The disguises."

Her husband raised one eyebrow. "You don't?" he asked.

Mrs. Cortez shrugged. "Okay, okay, I admit it," she said. "I've been dying to go on a mission again! I want to save the world!"

"Well, it looks like we'll get our chance," Mr. Cortez said. "Now that Donnagon and the other agents are missing."

Mrs. Cortez nodded. She had already been told about their new assignment. Donnagon was an old friend of theirs—a spy who worked for the same government agency as they did—the Office of Strategic Services, also called the OSS.

Donnagon and the others had probably been kidnapped by some evil group. Now Mr. and Mrs. Cortez were being asked to come out of retirement to find them.

"You know, honey, the spy thing is old," Mr. Cortez said. "If Devlin himself hadn't called me, I'd have turned down this assignment."

Devlin was head of the OSS.

"No way." Mrs. Cortez shook her head. "You're just as excited about this as I am."

Mr. Cortez smiled. "Well," he said as he put his fake mustache on, "maybe I am. Just a little."

Mrs. Cortez checked herself in the mirror again. She looked beautiful. With her short wavy brown hair and long legs, she was a perfect partner for her husband. Mr. Cortez had dark hair and a thin black mustache. His well-toned muscles stood out under his tight black T-shirt and pants.

Together, they looked like nothing could stop them.

"But we're parents now," Mr. Cortez said. "We really shouldn't be going on this mission. We're taking so many risks."

"I know," Mrs. Cortez said. "But we don't have any choice. Let's go!"

On their way out of the house, they stopped to say good-bye to the kids. Carmen and Juni were hanging out in the family room, playing a video game called RX Flight Simulator. Uncle Felix watched from a comfortable chair.

"We're leaving now," Mrs. Cortez called.

The kids were concentrating on the game. "Bye," they replied.

"Don't worry about us," Mrs. Cortez went on. "We're just going to take care of Aunt Gradenko." She winked at Uncle Felix and he winked back. He knew the truth about the spy mission. But the kids didn't notice. "We'll be gone only a few days."

"Okay," Carmen answered, without glancing up from the game.

"Don't you want to say good-bye, Juni?" Mrs. Cortez asked.

Juni started to come over to give his parents a hug. But then he noticed a clock on the wall. "Whoa! It's time for *Floop's Fooglies!*"

He whirled around and raced to the TV instead. His favorite kids' show was just coming on.

Mr. Cortez sighed. "Juni, why do you watch that show?" he asked.

Juni's eyes were eagerly glued to the set. "Because it's cool," he answered.

"But that's all you ever do," his dad said. "Play those video games, watch that show, and collect those Fooglie toys."

Juni hardly heard his dad. He was totally captivated by the program. It was set in Floop's castle. The show opened with a picture of a spooky castle on a rocky island somewhere in the middle of the ocean. Then a giant rainbow-colored sliding board appeared in the sky. The Fooglies—strange creatures with goofy, twisted, oversized heads and faces—came zooming down the slide.

One Fooglie had a blue head with scalloped edges. Another had a pointed lavender head. His mouth stretched sideways, as if someone had stuffed a hanger inside. The Fooglies all had large, lumpy bodies too.

They wore bright, colorful costumes and had weird smiles on their faces—but they didn't look happy. They looked scary and strange.

Mrs. Cortez turned to her husband. "Gregorio—we have to go."

"I know," Mr. Cortez said. But he bent over to pick up a drawing Juni had made. It was a picture of a Fooglie—but not a real one. It was Juni's own creation.

"Look at this," Mr. Cortez said softly to his wife.

"It's hideous. Why did he draw this?"

Mrs. Cortez looked at the Fooglie picture. It *was* scary and horrible.

"I don't know. Talk to him about it," Mrs. Cortez said, nodding toward Juni.

Mr. Cortez sighed. "I will. When we get back," he promised.

He put Juni's picture in his pocket. Then he glanced back at the TV screen.

Floop, the host of the TV show, was talking straight into the camera. He wore a fancy purple suit and a strange black glove on one hand. He appeared to be sitting on some clouds in a bright, sunny sky.

"Today we have a new character, boys and girls," Floop said. "We found him snooping around our castle last night. I'd like you all to meet— Donnamight!"

The camera zoomed in on the new Fooglie. Mr. Cortez's mouth dropped open. He shot a worried glance at his wife.

"Look," he said softly, nodding toward the new Fooglie on TV.

Together, Mr. and Mrs. Cortez stared at Donnamight. He had a strange head and roly-poly body, like the other Fooglies. He wore wild clothes. But there was something about him that looked very familiar.

Mr. Cortez took out a photograph of Donnagon, the missing OSS agent, from his pocket. He glanced at the photo, then at the TV screen.

"Wow," Mrs. Cortez said quietly. "If you put Donnagon in a blender with some colored clay . . . he might come out looking like that."

Mr. Cortez nodded. "I know."

Worried, he stared again at the TV screen. Could Floop be the villain who had kidnapped Donnagon? "Are you thinking what I'm thinking?" he asked his wife.

She nodded. "We'd better pay a visit to a certain TV show host."

CHAPTERTHREE

From his dark castle on the remote rocky island, Floop stared out at the ocean. He had just finished filming his TV show for the day. Now it was time to think about more important matters.

"Is he waiting for me?" Floop asked his right-hand man, Minion.

Minion nodded and squinted through thick glasses. "Yes, sir. Mr. Lisp is in the Grand Room."

"Very good," Floop said, nervously adjusting his purple vest. "Let's keep him waiting a bit longer."

"Do we dare?" Minion asked. "He's not very happy."

"I know," Floop said. He paced around the room, thinking. On his left hand he wore a strange black glove. In it he held an unusual ball of clay. He played with the clay, molding it into ugly shapes.

"Mr. Lisp wants you to deliver what you promised," Minion said. "He's waiting with all the other men who gave you money for the project."

"All right, all right," Floop said finally. "I'll talk to them."

He briskly marched into the Grand Room of his castle. The room was huge and dark, the ceilings arched. Mr. Lisp was seated in a metal chair, surrounded by a group of businessmen. Standing nearby were all the Fooglies that Floop had invented—including his newest one, Donnamight.

"Ah, Floop," Mr. Lisp said. "So glad you could join us."

"Good morning, gentlemen," Floop said, squeezing the ball of clay. "I see you've met the Fooglies."

Mr. Lisp frowned. "Yes," he said. "And I want an explanation. Are they what you spent our first billion dollars on?" he demanded.

"Well—" Floop began.

But Mr. Lisp interrupted him. "Year after year we've given you money!" he shouted. "You and a handful of other inventors. We counted on you to come up with new ideas, new technologies. Something creative and clever that we could use against the OSS. But instead, you invented these silly, costly . . . *things*."

"If you'll let me explain . . . " Floop tried to say.

Mr. Lisp narrowed his eyes. "You promised us an army, Mr. Floop. An army we could use to infiltrate the OSS. Instead, you've given us these . . . these . . . mutated secret agents. These *freaks!*"

Mr. Lisp marched over to the group of Fooglies.

He gestured toward Donnamight.

"What happened here?" Mr. Lisp demanded.

Floop looked embarrassed. "Well," he said. "We captured some OSS agents and went to work on them. But I'm afraid the mutation process turned their brains to mush. I haven't found much use for them, except as—"

"As what?" Mr. Lisp demanded.

"As characters on my children's TV show," Floop admitted. He sounded embarrassed.

"Hmmph. That ridiculous TV show!" Mr. Lisp said in disgust. "I'll bet that's where another billion of our money went to."

"The show is very popular with children. And very profitable," Floop said. "We've made a lot of money with the video games and Fooglie toys."

"Small change." Mr. Lisp shrugged. "We're not interested. We want an army—or our money back."

Mr. Lisp marched over to a large, hulking figure that looked like an inflated man. Its arms were long and thick, but instead of hands it had only two giant thumbs. And in place of a head there was—a third thumb! When Mr. Lisp looked around, he saw a whole group of them. They were dressed in red, stretchy one-piece jumpsuits.

"What are these?" he asked Floop.

"Another one of my inventions," Floop answered. "They're called Thumb Thumbs. They're very good robots. Except for—"

Mr. Lisp tossed a book to the Thumb Thumb.

The robot dropped it on the floor.

"Except for that," Floop said. "They're all thumbs."

"Useless!" Mr. Lisp said, throwing up his arms. "We've given you money, and you've failed!"

"No!" Floop said, raising his voice. "Not yet anyway. I know I've had some failures in the past. But I think I've finally come up with the answer. The breakthrough in espionage that you've been looking for."

All the businessmen in the room grew quiet.

"Really?" Mr. Lisp glanced around. "Where?"

"I'll show you," Floop answered. "Just watch that door. In ten seconds, an awesome power will enter this room. You will have only a moment to disarm it, Mr. Lisp."

Floop backed away from the door. So did the other businessmen. Mr. Lisp got ready to fight.

"Ten, nine, eight . . . " Floop counted down.

When ten seconds were up, the door flew open. A young boy leaped into the room with a long stick in his hands. He came at Mr. Lisp.

Mr. Lisp looked confused. "Johnny?" He lowered his arms.

In a flash, the boy leaped over Mr. Lisp and knocked him to the ground.

"Ha!" Floop cried. "See? You hesitated! And he won!"

"But I had to hesitate," Mr. Lisp said, frowning. "He's my *son*."

Floop grinned slyly from ear to ear. "Look closely. Are you sure?"

Mr. Lisp peered into the boy's eyes—and saw that they were electronic.

"See?" Floop said. "He's not your son—he's mine. I mean, I invented him."

Angrily, Mr. Lisp got to his feet. "*This* is your big idea? Robot kids who look like my own kid? What good is that?"

"Oh, but they won't *all* look like your son," Floop answered.

Floop snapped his fingers, and another robot child entered the Grand Room. This one was a girl. And she looked exactly like the daughter of the president of the United States! She marched straight up to Mr. Lisp and flipped him onto the floor again.

Lisp got up more slowly this time. "Hmmm," he said. "The president's daughter? That *is* clever, Mr. Floop."

The businessmen in the room nodded with pleasure.

"Yes," Floop agreed. "Think of the power you'll have if you can gain entry into the homes of all the richest and most powerful families in the world."

Mr. Lisp's eyes glowed with interest. "Go on," he said.

"I have a whole army of them," Floop explained. "Robots that look exactly like the sons and daughters of world leaders . . . bankers . . . corporate leaders.

They can take out money from bank accounts, steal business secrets . . . the possibilities are mind-boggling!"

The robot girl took Mr. Lisp's wallet and handed the money in it to Floop.

"Thank you," Floop told her. Then he went on. "They have the strength of an army—combined with the intelligence and trickery of the world's best spies. It's all rolled into a tiny package I call Spy Kids."

"Fantastic!" Mr. Lisp declared. He bent down to talk to one of the robots. It was the one that looked like his own son. "Tell me, Spy Kid. If you're so smart, how do you know when someone is lying?"

"Gib jub gub-gub glee. Wub wub mucky-mucky, hig wag bug-dug wob," the Spy Kid said.

Mr. Lisp shot a dagger-filled glare at Floop. "What's that garbage supposed to mean?"

"Uh . . . the Spy Kids are not quite finished," Floop answered. "They're missing one important element."

"What is that?" Lisp asked.

"Their brains," Floop replied.

Lisp threw up his hands in fury. "These buckets of bolts will never pass as children!" he shouted.

"Oh, dear," Floop said. He nervously wiped his forehead with the money from Mr. Lisp's wallet.

"Look," Lisp said. "I'll give you two days. Just two days! If you don't make these robots work, and deliver my army that you promised, I'll ruin you! Do you understand? Ruin you—and everything else in this rattrap of a castle!"

Then he stormed out. The other businessmen followed right behind him.

Floop watched them go. Mr. Lisp had seemed really mad. Floop wondered how he would find a way to make his Spy Kids work for real in only two days.

CHAPTERFOUR

"**S**hhh! You'll wake Uncle Felix!" Carmen whispered to Juni the next morning.

Juni glanced into the family room. Uncle Felix was asleep on the couch. The TV was on, but the sound was muted.

"He's snoring," Juni said. "He's wrecked from letting us stay up watching TV all night."

"All night?" Carmen laughed. "You were asleep by eleven, Bedtime Boy."

She poured herself a bowl of Fooglie cereal. The little crunchy pieces were shaped like the colorful characters on Floop's TV show.

"You fell asleep first," Juni said.

"Did not," Carmen argued. She picked up a handful of dry cereal and threw it at her brother.

All at once, a loud beeping alarm went off. Carmen and Juni both jumped.

"What did you do?" Carmen said, glancing

around. Sirens screeched throughout the house.

Juni stared at the microwave. The sound seemed to be coming from there. The microwave's window said "RED ALERT!" and the alarm was blaring.

Immediately, Uncle Felix sat bolt upright. The clock beside him was blasting an alarm too. It said "RED ALERT!" where the time should have been. And the TV picture had totally disappeared. The words "RED ALERT!" flashed in huge letters across the screen.

"Oh, my gosh!" Uncle Felix shouted.

"What's going on? Is it a fire drill?" Juni asked. "What should we do?"

"No!" Felix cried, leaping up and racing to a closet. "It's not a drill!"

In a panic, he quickly grabbed three silver-and-black backpacks. While the alarm blared, he tossed two of them to the Cortez kids.

"Put these on quickly!" Uncle Felix ordered. "There's no time!"

"But—" Juni started to say.

Suddenly, the alarms stopped. The words "RED ALERT!" disappeared from the TV screen. Instead, the television showed a view of what was happening outside the Cortez house.

Cars were screeching into the driveway.

Hooded men were running toward the front door.

A helicopter was circling overhead.

"What's happening?" Carmen demanded.

Uncle Felix's face grew even more serious. "Follow me," he said, hurrying down a hallway. "There's a lot for you to know and little time to explain."

"Uncle Felix!" Carmen called, trying to keep up with him.

He stopped and turned around. "The first thing you need to know is that I'm not your uncle," he said. Then he reached up and pulled off his big bushy black mustache.

It was fake!

Carmen and Juni both gasped.

"Listen to me," Felix said quickly. "Your parents are international spies. Good ones. They've been mostly retired for the past nine years, but now they're back in the game."

"Are you kidding?" Carmen asked. Juni's mouth was hanging open.

"No." Felix talked fast as he hurried to a bookcase at the end of the hall. He started pulling books and objects off the shelves. "I was assigned to protect you. But something has gone wrong. Terribly wrong. Your parents are in trouble. I have to take you to the safe house."

"A safe what?" Carmen asked.

Her head was spinning. She couldn't believe any of this was true! But it had to be. The alarms sounded so real. And the words "RED ALERT!" had flashed on practically everything in the house!

"A safe house is a place where you can hide from

bad guys," Felix explained. "We've got to hurry."

"My parents can't be spies," Carmen said. "They're not cool enough to be spies."

Felix didn't answer. He had finally found what he was looking for on the bookshelf. Hidden behind some books was a doorknob. When Felix turned it, the whole bookshelf swung open.

There was a secret passage behind it!

"Wow, *that's* cool!" Juni exclaimed.

The helicopter sounds outside the house grew louder.

"Hurry!" Felix urged, pushing the kids into the dark passageway. Then he stepped inside and pulled the heavy bookshelf door closed behind them.

A small light came on in the hall.

"But how are our parents getting back home?" Carmen asked.

"They're not," Felix answered grimly. "I'll have to go find them myself."

In a flash he pulled a small handheld device out of his backpack.

"What's that?" Juni asked.

"A locator," Felix explained. He squinted at it. "According to this, your parents are being taken to either Asia . . . or . . . "

He turned his head sideways to look at it. Then he turned the device around a few times.

" . . . South America," he said. Uncle Felix didn't sound too sure. "Come on. We have no time! We have to keep moving!"

He pushed Carmen and Juni farther along the hallway and opened another door at the end. It was a closet filled with clothes. Felix put the locator device and his own backpack on the floor.

"Wait in there!" he ordered the kids, his voice rising. "Don't move. I'll be right back!"

In a clothes closet? Carmen thought. How safe was that?

"What if you're not right back?" she called after him.

Felix ran down the hallway, back toward the main part of the house.

"Push the blue button to seal the door, then hit the green button to go!" he yelled.

Then he disappeared through the bookcase, closing it behind him.

The hallway was quiet.

"Is this a joke?" Juni asked, his voice shaky.

"I don't think so," Carmen answered. She bit her lip.

Slowly, they both lifted their backpacks and put them on. The backpack was too big and heavy for Juni. The weight of it made him fall onto his back.

"Whoa!" he cried, trying to stand up again. He reached out to pull himself up by holding on to Carmen.

"Get your warty hands off me!" she told him, jerking away.

When she saw her brother's face, Carmen was

sorry she had snapped like that. It was filled with fear.

"Did you hear that?" he asked.

She nodded and listened. There were all kinds of noises outside the house. And *inside* too. Glass breaking. Furniture smashing. Yelling. The helicopter engine roaring.

Juni glanced around the closet and pushed the clothes aside.

"Carmen, look!" he said.

Behind the clothes was a small pod-shaped vehicle. On the side, it said "Super Guppy." It looked like a fish-shaped car, with two seats. The door to the pod was open.

"Wow." Carmen climbed inside.

The instant she sat down, a monitor inside the pod lit up. It showed a view from a camera mounted inside the house. Now she could see what was happening to Uncle Felix.

Juni climbed into the pod beside his sister. "Oh, man!" he cried when he saw the monitor.

Some huge men dressed all in black were surrounding Felix. They had thick arms and oversize heads. Their hands and faces were covered with black gloves and hoods.

Felix fought back, karate-style, kicking the huge attackers onto their backs.

"Look out, Felix!" Juni cried as another one of the thugs attacked their fake uncle.

Felix spun around and kicked the chunky man

out of the way. Then he ran up to the camera. He knew Juni and Carmen could see him.

"You'll have to go to the safe house without me!" he cried. "Go *now*!"

Behind Felix, another door burst open. Someone—or something—else was coming to fight him.

"Find the OSS!" Felix told the kids. "Tell them that the *Third Brain lives*! You're our only hope! You must find your parents before . . . "

Then the picture on the monitor went dead.

Carmen's heart was racing. She looked at her brother. Juni was nearly frozen in shock.

"Press the blue and green buttons!" Carmen shouted.

Juni shook his head. "We can't leave Felix behind," he said.

A loud crash startled them both. It was the book-case doorway. Someone had crashed through it! Footsteps pounded toward them.

"Oh, yes, we can! We have to go—now!" Carmen shouted. "Blue to close, then green to go! Quick!"

Juni looked around frantically, trying to find the buttons. Carmen jumped out of the pod to grab Felix's bag and the locator device.

A green light on the control panel flashed on and off.

"Green!" Juni cried. "Here it is!"

He pushed the button.

Instantly, the pod began to move—leaving Carmen behind!

"No!" Carmen cried. "Blue button first! Juni, wait for me!"

CHAPTER FIVE

"**C**armen!" Juni called to his sister as the Super Guppy began to launch.

Carmen leaped forward into the pod—just in time!

"You never do anything right, Juni!" Carmen yelled at him. "Blue, *then* green! You were supposed to seal the door first!"

The pod rocketed through a launching tunnel, its door still open. Carmen held on for dear life.

With one foot, she reached out and kicked the blue button.

"Hang on!" she shouted to Juni. The pod shot out of the launching tunnel—and straight into midair!

Their family's house was built into the side of a cliff, overlooking the ocean. The tunnel opened right over the water.

"We're flying!" Juni cried.

Carmen glanced out the pod's big front window. "No, we're not," she said, swallowing hard. "We're . . . falling!"

SPLASH! A moment later, the pod landed hard in the water. Carmen and Juni held their breath, wondering if it would sink.

"It floats!" Juni cried in relief.

Suddenly, an engine whirled. The Super Guppy sped forward across the surface of the water, racing like a supercharged speedboat.

Then, all by itself, the top window of the pod peeled open like a sunroof. Carmen and Juni stood up and stuck their heads out to look around.

"Oh, no," Juni moaned.

"Yikes!" Carmen cried.

Three or four speedboats had been waiting at the base of the cliff by the Cortez house. They were filled with more of those black-hooded men. Now they zoomed across the water, chasing the Super Guppy.

The pod automatically sped up.

"What are you doing?" Juni shouted at Carmen.

"Nothing!" she cried. "It's driving itself!"

Juni ducked back into the pod and grabbed the wheel. "They're catching up to us!" he yelled. "We've got to get away."

He tried to turn the pod, but it was hard to control.

"Don't touch anything!" Carmen shouted to him. Too late.

"Manual override engaged," Juni heard the pod's computer say. That meant the driving was totally up to him.

The pod bounced hard on the water, rocking wildly. Then it swerved sideways, almost hitting a nearby fishing boat.

"You idiot!" Carmen shouted. She pushed Juni out of the way and took control of the pod.

Water splashed up everywhere as the Super Guppy whirled around. Bouncing on the water, Carmen made the pod leap over the fishing boat, then zoom out of the way.

Juni held on tight. Through the window, he and Carmen saw the speedboats slam into the fishing boat. The guys in black and their boats all flew up in the air and landed in the water far behind them.

"Phew!" Juni said. "That was close. So now we're okay, right?"

"No," Carmen said. "This thing was pro-grammed to take us to the safe house—until *you* took over. Now we'll never get there!"

CHAPTER SIX

"That's him? The great Gregorio Cortez?" Floop asked.

Minion nodded. "The best spy the OSS has to offer, sir."

The two of them sat in the castle's control room, surrounded by television monitors. Each monitor displayed a view of a different part of the castle. On one screen, Floop watched as Mr. and Mrs. Cortez were led down a long hallway to a cell, deep in the castle's dungeon.

As Mr. Cortez passed one cell, he glanced inside and saw Donnamight. From the look on Mr. Cortez's face, Floop knew what the super spy was thinking. Could that creature—Donnamight—be his old friend Donnagon?

"How did we capture them, sir?" Minion asked.

"It was easy," Floop replied. He leaned closer to the monitor. "They sped right into our trap."

The Cortezes' hands were tightly tied behind their backs. Guarding them were more of the strange men in black.

"Why don't you guys lose the masks?" Mrs. Cortez said to her captors. "We're all friends here."

After a slight pause, the guards lifted the masks off their heads. Their heads were—thumbs!

Mr. and Mrs. Cortez both flinched at the Thumb Thumbs' creepy appearance.

"We've taken all of their maps, gadgets, and communicators away," Minion told Floop. "We also found a bizarre drawing in Mr. Cortez's pocket. I wonder what *this* means."

He handed the drawing to Floop. It was the hideous Fooglie that Juni had drawn.

"Hmmm," Floop said. "This may come in handy."

"What are you going to do to our two prisoners?" Minion asked.

"I'm not sure," Floop answered. As usual, he held a small ball of clay in his hand, molding it into some kind of shape. "I suspect Cortez knows something that could help us supply brains to our Spy Kids army. But he's too dangerous to trust."

"Yes," Minion agreed, nodding. "It's interesting. Gregorio Cortez is the only agent we knew without a weakness. But now he has three of them."

Floop's head snapped up. "What do you mean, Minion?" Floop asked.

Minion gave his boss an evil grin. "His wife and

two children, of course," he answered.

"Ahhh! Then we must capture his children, mustn't we?" Floop said. Now he was smiling too.

"We're already working on that," Minion replied.

"Good." Floop stared down at the ball of clay in his hands. He molded it some more, then held it up next to the monitor that showed Mr. Cortez's face. "Not bad, eh, Minion?"

Minion shot Floop an admiring glance. "The things you can do with that ball of clay, sir. You're an absolute genius! Have I told you that?"

Floop smiled once again. "Many times, Minion. Many times. And this next project may be my most brilliant creation ever."

CHAPTERSEVEN

"Where are we going?" Juni shouted to Carmen as the pod sped across the water.

"I don't know!" she cried. "You're the one who put it in manual override! You messed everything up!"

"Well, do something!" Juni cried. "How do you put it back?"

"Back to what?" Carmen asked.

"Autopilot!" Juni said.

The minute he said the word, the computer obeyed. "Autopilot is engaged," the computer voice told them. BINGO!

Carmen sighed with relief. She and Juni stuck their heads out through the sunroof again. All at once, the pod sped up, racing straight for an island in the distance.

"How does this thing work?" Juni asked. "Do

you think it's going there on purpose?"

"I guess so," Carmen said with a shrug.

Suddenly, the sunroof started to close.

"Duck!" Carmen ordered Juni.

The two of them dove back into the pod. Above them, the door sealed itself tightly. Then, to Carmen and Juni's amazement, the pod dove under the water, like a submarine!

"Wow," Juni said. "Where are we going?"

Before his sister could answer, he pushed a button on the control panel.

"Don't touch anything!" Carmen screamed at him.

But it was too late. This time, a cover on the front of the pod slid open smoothly. Behind it was a huge window. It revealed the whole ocean in front of them. "Welcome to the N-I-X Super Guppy," the computer said.

The pod zoomed through a beautiful tropical reef filled with colorful fish and gorgeous green seaweed.

Carmen watched, amazed. This was the most fantastic view of the ocean she had ever seen.

Then she spotted something that made her heart skip a beat. Large black shapes with pointed fins on their backs were cutting through the water like torpedoes.

Sharks!

"Juni, close your eyes!" Carmen ordered him.

She knew her little brother would freak if he saw

an ocean full of sharks heading for them.

"Why?" Juni asked. But he squeezed his eyes shut tight.

"Just keep 'em shut, all right?" Carmen said.

Her heart hammered as the pod moved through a pack of thirty or more hungry sharks. When it seemed like they were out of danger, she let Juni open his eyes again.

"I just don't want you crying all over me," she explained, trying to sound tough.

Juni looked confused. But Carmen was staring at the control panel now, taking in all the buttons. One of them said Play. She reached out and pushed it.

"Hello, children," their father said. His voice was coming from a monitor in front of them.

Carmen and Juni stared hard at the video their parents had recorded.

"If you're watching this, it means that something has happened to your mother, myself, or to both of us," Mr. Cortez said. "You see, life is full of choices. And sometimes things end up going unsaid—"

"What we're trying to say," Mrs. Cortez interrupted, "is that your father and I are secret agents of the OSS. We once lived lives of great danger. If you're watching this, it means that danger has returned."

Juni leaned closer to Carmen.

"Do as Felix says," Mrs. Cortez continued. "He is there to help you. And don't worry. Hopefully, soon we'll be together again."

"Don't be afraid, Juni," Mr. Cortez added. "And, Carmen—you're responsible for your brother now. Take care of him."

"Oh, great." Carmen sighed. But she knew it was true. She had to watch out for Juni. He was only eight.

"Remember, we're counting on you," Mr. Cortez said. "See you soon."

Mrs. Cortez held her hand up close to the camera. So did her husband. Then they both turned their silver wedding rings around. The letters "OSS" were etched into the other side of the rings. Then the tape ended.

"Wow!" Carmen whispered. But she felt a little tightness at the back of her throat. She glanced at Juni. He looked worried and afraid.

"We're never going to see them again, are we?" he asked his sister softly.

"I don't know, Juni," she answered honestly. "I just don't know."

CHAPTEREIGHT

"I knew this would happen!" Mr. Cortez complained to his wife as they struggled to get free.

The two of them were tied up, back to back.

"And *this* is why I never wanted to go on another mission," he added.

"You're blaming *me*?" Mrs. Cortez was shocked. "An hour ago, you were happy to be back in the spy game!"

"An hour ago, I was not a prisoner of war!" Mr. Cortez shot back.

True, Mrs. Cortez thought. "So we're a little rusty," she admitted to her husband. She twisted her hands, still struggling against the ropes.

"If something happens to us, who will take care of the children?" Mr. Cortez asked.

Mrs. Cortez didn't answer. She didn't even want to think about that.

"Look, I know we didn't plan to get captured," she said. "But at least this is *one* way to find out who's been kidnapping those OSS agents. And if I can . . . just get the right pressure . . . "

She twisted her hands harder. Suddenly, there was a click.

"Ah-ha!" Mrs. Cortez cried triumphantly.

A thin red laser beam shot out of her ring. She pointed it toward the ropes around her wrists. The laser burned brightly through, and the ropes fell away.

"I've still got it!" Mrs. Cortez announced proudly as she jumped up, free.

"No wonder I fell in love with you!" Mr. Cortez said, smiling.

Mrs. Cortez cut the ropes for her husband. Then Mr. Cortez pulled a thin metal blade out of his fake mustache. He quickly used it to pick the lock on their cell.

A few moments later, the two of them crept through the castle hallway.

"That's weird," Mrs. Cortez said. "This place is deserted."

She glanced into the cells they had passed earlier—especially the one where she and her husband had seen Donnamight.

All of the cells were empty now.

"There aren't even any guards," Mr. Cortez said, frowning. "Maybe they realized who we were and gave up," he joked.

"Not likely," Mrs. Cortez told him.

They rounded a corner into a long hallway. The castle walls arched high over their heads. As the two of them paused for half an instant, deciding which way to go, the floor beneath them began to vibrate.

"What . . . ?" Mr. Cortez began.

A moment later, the floor began to open. It split right down the middle, revealing a huge gaping pit below.

Now Mr. and Mrs. Cortez were on opposite sides of the deep chasm!

Mrs. Cortez sighed. "Remember when we could sense danger a mile away?" she said to her husband.

"Those were the days," Mr. Cortez agreed with a nod.

He took a few steps back. Then he ran toward her, ready to leap across the opening. But as he did, the floor opened even wider! There was no way he could make it across!

He jumped anyway.

"Sweetheart—no!" Mrs. Cortez cried when her husband was in midair.

Mr. Cortez fell—and landed with a thud on the floor. The "pit" in the middle of the floor was a fake—an optical illusion. Probably a computer special effect.

"Huh?" Mr. Cortez said, slightly stunned. His face was smashed against a pane of glass. Below it was the computer illusion. "Oh. Very clever," he said in a grumpy voice. "Very clever indeed."

He pulled himself up, and together he and his wife tiptoed farther along the hall. Suddenly, they heard the sound of snapping fingers.

What's that? Mrs. Cortez wondered. She shot her husband a questioning glance.

The answer was clear in his eyes: Time to hide!

Quickly, the two of them felt around for a doorknob, opened it, and slipped inside.

Phew! Mrs. Cortez thought. At least now we're . . .

"Whoa!" she said, letting the word escape out loud.

Without realizing it, they had stumbled into Floop's Virtual Room. It was a fantasy place, a world filled with bizarre computer images. Upside-down landscapes. Wildly blinding colors. Everything spinning.

The two spies both felt dizzy from the sights. They whirled around again, searching for the door they had come in, but it was—gone.

"Unbelievable," Mr. Cortez said, making his way around the room.

As they walked, the images kept changing. First they found themselves in a desert . . . then a lush and beautiful garden. Suddenly, the garden transformed into a gorgeous bank of clouds, with the sun setting far ahead.

"Very clever," Mr. Cortez said, still grumpy. "Very . . . "

Uh-oh, he thought suddenly. How can we be

walking on clouds? That's impossible.

In a flash, he and his wife found themselves falling . . . falling . . .

Right through a trapdoor in the floor!

CHAPTER NINE

"Don't worry about Mom and Dad," Carmen tried to comfort her brother. "They're famous spies. They can take care of themselves. I think."

Juni nodded, but he didn't look as if he totally believed her. He stared out the window of the Super Guppy. Straight ahead, he and Carmen could see a beat-up wooden shack on a deserted island. The pod was clearly headed for that shack.

"That's a safe house?" Carmen muttered.

"Doesn't look very safe to me," Juni replied.

The Super Guppy finally came to a rest near some rocks. Carmen and Juni climbed out. They walked up to the shack's door and stared at it.

"How are we supposed to get in?" Carmen said.

To her amazement, a computerized voice answered. "Name?" it asked.

"Carmen Cortez," Carmen answered.

"Your *full* name," the computer said.

"I don't use my full name. It's too long," Carmen snapped.

"Your full name, please," the computer repeated.

"Carmen Elizabeth Juanita Echo Sky Brava Cortez," Carmen answered. "Are you happy?"

The computer didn't reply. But the door immediately unlocked and swung open.

"Cool," Carmen said. Now she realized why her parents had given her so many names. "My name is a pass code!"

Once inside the shack, she and Juni gazed around. From the outside, it had looked pretty shabby. But inside was a different story. Everything was high-tech! They were completely surrounded by all kinds of metal lockers, command panels, droid robots, and pieces of spy communications equipment.

"I get the big bed!" Carmen declared before her brother could think of it.

Then she frowned and gazed around the room. Was there even a bed in here?

She ran to look at the kitchen area. There was a refrigerator, but it was empty. So were all the cupboards.

"How safe is a safe house if there's nothing to eat?" Carmen mumbled as she closed the fridge door.

Then she heard something moving. Shifting around. She opened the door again.

Somehow, the fridge had instantly filled itself with food! "Awesome!" Carmen cried.

Actually, it wasn't really food. Most of it was freeze-dried packets of food. Carmen and Juni had to stick them in a machine that added water, to make it edible.

For the next hour, the two of them explored the safe house. They found all kinds of cool things—action jumpsuits in their own kid sizes, wristwatch communicators, techno-spy sunglasses, and a small black leather instruction book called *How to Be a Spy*.

Carmen immediately opened the book and started reading.

Meanwhile, Juni tested out the gadgets. He tried on the wristwatch communicator. A loud squealing noise filled the room.

"Ouch! You're standing too close!" Carmen scolded him. "It's for *long distance* communication, genius. Got that?"

Juni ignored her and slipped on the spy sunglasses. "Gross," he said.

"What do you see?" she asked.

"You." Juni smiled, proud of his own joke.

"Very funny," she said. "But that's not how they work. Focus your eyes closer. On the glasses themselves."

She slipped on an identical pair, then hit a button on her wristwatch.

Immediately, computer readouts appeared on

the lenses of both sets of glasses.

"Whoa! Maps and stuff!" Juni exclaimed.

"It's some kind of database," Carmen said. "Don't move your eyes too much, or you'll get a splitting headache."

Juni stared at the readouts while Carmen explored the rest of the safe house. On a table she found a wedding album with pictures of her mom and dad. They were dressed as spies at their own wedding.

"Juni! You know that bedtime story Mom always tells? It was *their* story. Mom and Dad were the spies who got married," Carmen said, amazed.

Juni glanced over her shoulder at the photos of his parents. He looked sad. Carmen knew exactly what he was thinking.

What if they never saw their parents again?

Don't think about that, she told herself. And don't let Juni think about it either! To distract him, she began to read the spy book aloud.

"How to be a spy," she said. "Number one: A good spy always uses his head. Got that, Juni?"

"Yeah," he grumbled. He knew his sister was making fun of him because he was always making mistakes.

"Number two: A good spy never falls in love," Carmen said. She frowned. "At least I *think* that's what it says. It's been crossed out."

"Mom and Dad should have told us about all this stuff!" Juni complained.

"Oh, yeah? Do *you* tell *them* everything?" Carmen said.

That shut her brother up. Carmen knew it would. Juni had lots of secrets he didn't want his parents to know about. Like the fact that he didn't have too many friends at school. He made up names of friends—kids who didn't exist—so his parents wouldn't worry about him.

Of course, Carmen had a few secrets too—about the times she skipped school, for instance. But that was only because she was hungry for adventure.

I'm just like Mom, Carmen thought suddenly.

She went back to the spy rules. "A good spy has *no fear*," Carmen read aloud. "Sorry, Juni. Guess you can't be a spy. Ha-ha."

She glanced up, expecting him to punch her or something. But her little brother was busy with a different problem. He had accidentally handcuffed himself to a silver metal lunch box.

"Uh, Carmen?" he said helplessly.

"I don't have the key," she said, shrugging. "Go knock it against something."

Juni followed her advice. He swung the lunch box hard at a wall. It bounced back and hit him in the head!

"Ow!" he cried, flying to the ground.

"A good spy uses deception instead of *force*," Carmen went on, reading another rule.

Juni picked himself up and shook his head. He felt dizzy.

"And here's the most important one," Carmen said. "A good spy tries to put himself—or herself—in the mind-set of the opponent."

"Huh?" Juni said.

"That means we have to think like the bad guys if we're going to survive," his sister explained.

From her pack, she pulled out the locator device that Felix had used when they were back home.

"This will tell us how to find Mom and Dad," Carmen told Juni, turning the locator on. "And that's exactly what we're going to do."

"We are?" Juni asked.

Carmen gestured to all the spy stuff. "We've got communicators, a database, a locating device, and an instruction manual. It's up to us to find the OSS, like Felix said. And to rescue Mom and Dad. Are you with me?"

Juni's head was still spinning from hitting himself with the lunch box. He couldn't think very well. All he could do was say "Okay."

"Great," Carmen said. "Then let's go!"

CHAPTER TEN

"Ow!" Mrs. Cortez cried out. She and her husband had fallen through the trapdoor in Floop's castle into the room below. And they'd landed smack in the middle of the long dining table in Floop's Grand Room.

Floop sat at the head of the table. He clicked his stopwatch. "Hmmph! It took you exactly fifteen minutes to escape!" he declared. "I thought famous spies like you would get here faster! Oh, well. At least now we can eat."

He picked up a spoon and began eating some kind of bright blue soup. All the other bowls at the table were filled with colorful soupy mixtures. Some were bright red, some yellow, some green.

"So you're Floop," Mr. Cortez said. He recognized the host of Juni's favorite TV show.

"Ah, you watch my show?" Floop said. He sounded pleased.

"My son does," Mr. Cortez said quietly.

"Does he? Wonderful!" Floop declared. "Maybe Juni and your daughter, Carmen, will be joining us soon!"

Mr. Cortez glanced at his wife. They were top secret spies, so they knew never to let their feelings show. But inside, they were both wondering the same thing: How did Floop find out their children's names? And did it mean that the children were in danger?

Mr. Cortez didn't like being threatened. He started to lunge at Floop, but Floop held up his hand.

"Careful," he warned. "I snap my fingers . . . "

He nodded toward the Thumb Thumbs standing nearby.

" . . . and my fingers will snap you!"

The inventor leaned back in his chair and grinned, pleased with himself and his little joke.

Okay, Mr. Cortez thought. We can't fight our way out of this mess. Yet. But we *can* find out what Floop wants.

His wife was thinking the same thing.

"Where are the other OSS agents you've taken?" she demanded. "Why have you kidnapped them? And what do you want with us?"

Floop smiled. "Twelve years ago, those agents were part of an OSS research team," he explained. "They were trying to create an artificial intelligence filled with all the best spy secrets. But instead of finishing the project, they destroyed it! And no matter how hard I try, I just can't seem to convince them to re-create it. So . . . I've had to punish them."

Floop waved to the Thumb Thumbs. A moment later, the Fooglies were led into the room.

Mrs. Cortez gasped. The Fooglies were so . . . weird! In fact, Floop's whole castle reminded her of a circus gone wrong. There were bright colors and funny playful pieces of furniture everywhere. But most of the Fooglies were twisted and strange.

Worst of all, she recognized them. They were the missing **OSS** agents! But what had Floop done to them? They had been transformed into mutants.

"This is what happens when you refuse to help Floop!" Floop announced.

"I don't see how we can help you," Mrs. Cortez said. "The OSS destroyed the research."

"Oh, but there is one person who can rebuild that artificial intelligence system," Floop said. "Isn't there—Mr. *Cortez?*"

Mrs. Cortez shot her husband an angry glare. "What is he talking about?" she asked.

"We had the thing working," Mr. Cortez admitted. "When I was at the OSS. We called it the Ten Brains System. It was a series of artificial brains—as smart as any spy."

Mrs. Cortez couldn't believe that her husband had kept this a secret all these years. "Why didn't you tell me?" she whispered.

"I'm sorry. I wanted to protect you," he

explained. "You and the children."

"So will you rebuild the system for me?" Floop demanded.

"I wouldn't remember how," Mr. Cortez lied.

"I take that as a definite no," Floop said.

He pushed a button near the edge of the table. A TV monitor on the wall flickered on. On the screen, Mr. and Mrs. Cortez could see Felix being held prisoner somewhere inside Floop's castle. He was tied up and strapped to a chair. Wires were attached to his head.

Floop was playing with a ball of clay. He molded it into a copy of Felix's face. But then he twisted the model into something hideous and horrible.

He pushed another button. There was a flash of light on the screen as a jolt of electricity shot into Felix's head. A moment later, Felix was transformed into a sickening Fooglie. He looked just like the ball of clay in Floop's hands!

"This is what happens to people who try to resist me," Floop said.

Mr. Cortez was horrified by what Floop had done. But he wasn't going to be bullied.

"I'll never build anything for you," he told Floop. "No matter what kind of monster you make me!"

"Fine," Floop replied with an evil laugh. "But what about the monsters that I'll make of your children?"

Mrs. Cortez's mouth dropped open.

Mr. Cortez's heart pounded. Floop was going to

hurt Juni and Carmen!

He crossed his arms over his chest, trying to look tough.

But Floop simply laughed and pushed a third button. At once, Mr. and Mrs. Cortez fell through another trapdoor in the floor!

When they were gone, Floop turned to his right-hand man.

"Minion!" he snapped. "Don't you think it would be much better to threaten our guests with the children after we actually *had* them?"

"I'm working on it," Minion promised. "Don't worry—we'll have both Cortez kids very soon."

CHAPTERELEVEN

"**S**o how are we going to find Mom and Dad?" Juni asked Carmen.

"I'm not sure," Carmen admitted. "But I have an idea."

She showed her brother the wedding photo album. In one picture, their father stood beside his best man. On the back of the photo, there was writing. She read the best man's name—Machete.

"This guy Machete was at Mom and Dad's wedding," Carmen said. "And check out all the spy stuff in here. It's made by a company called Machete. It must be his."

Juni picked up the locator device and spy glasses. Sure enough, he saw the Machete mark and an address.

"Cool," Juni said. "So maybe Mr. Machete can help us?"

"That's what I'm hoping," Carmen said with a nod.

"Great. Then let's go," Juni said. He started toward the door. But before he and Carmen reached it, there was a knock from outside.

"Carmen? Juni?" a voice called.

Carmen froze. Who could be knocking on a safe house door in the middle of nowhere? she wondered. And how did the person know their names?

She tiptoed to the door and peeked out the peephole.

A beautiful woman with long wavy dark hair stood outside. She was dressed all in black. Behind her were several men in suits.

"I'm Ms. Gradenko," the woman said through the door. "We work for your parents."

Gradenko? Carmen thought. Hold on. This sounded fishy. Didn't her mom say she and Juni had an aunt named Gradenko?

"I can understand if you don't remember me," Ms. Gradenko said. "You were just a baby when we first met."

Before Carmen could decide what to do, the locked door opened.

"Remember me now?" the woman said. She smiled sweetly as she forced her way into the safe house.

"We're not supposed to let strangers into our house," Juni said.

"Right! But I'm not a stranger," Ms. Gradenko cooed in a syrupy voice. "I have a key. See? We're all on the same side."

I don't know about that, Carmen thought. Her head whirled as she tried to decide whether or not to trust this woman.

And what about those men with Ms. Gradenko? They had swooped into the safe house and were looking at everything.

Carmen shot Juni a worried glance. But then she noticed Ms. Gradenko's bracelet. It was a silver chain with a curved silver plate. The letters *OSS* were stamped on it.

"Mom had a bracelet like that," Carmen muttered, staring at it.

"Yes. It's standard for OSS agents," Ms. Gradenko said.

"OSS? So you work with my parents?" Carmen asked.

"Yes." Ms. Gradenko smiled. "Now, this is very important, so please listen carefully," she went on. "In the past year, several OSS agents have been taken prisoner. We believe that your parents have now been captured as well."

"By who?" Juni asked.

"Well, your father was able to send us one last message before he disappeared," she answered. "Here it is."

She held up a piece of paper. There were only five letters on it:

F-l-o-o-p.

Juni looked shocked. "No way," he said. "Not Fabulous Floop! He would never do that!"

"He's not that fabulous," Ms. Gradenko said. "I'm afraid he's been up to no good for quite a while."

She pulled out some pictures of the Fooglies and showed them to Juni. "Recognize these?" she asked Juni.

"Sure. Floop's Fooglies!" Juni said. "I collect all the toys."

Ms. Gradenko showed Juni and Carmen some photos of the missing OSS agents. "Well, those Fooglies used to look like *this*—before Floop mutated them," she said.

Juni's mouth fell open. "Really?" he asked in a small voice.

Ms. Gradenko nodded.

"Will he do that to Mom and Dad?" Carmen asked.

"Oh, definitely," the woman said. "Unless we can stop him. Now, think, children. Floop is trying to find something that your father helped develop when he worked for the OSS."

"What is it?" Carmen asked.

"We don't know." Ms. Gradenko sighed. "That's why we need your help. If there's anything you can remember . . . maybe something your parents said at dinner, or something you heard on the phone . . . anything at all."

"The Third Brain lives," Carmen muttered, remembering what Felix had told them.

"What?" Ms. Gradenko's eyes lit up.

Carmen and Juni were two regular kids. They thought their parents were regular parents. Until. . . .

Their parents were kidnapped! And Carmen and
Juni found out their mom and dad were really
secret agents . . .

. . . being held by the wicked techno-wizard, Floop.

Floop and his sidekick, Minion, with the help of their robot army of kids, planned to take over the world!

There was only one thing for them to do . . .
become spies themselves and save their parents!

Becoming a spy was a lot harder than it looked.
There were a million rules to follow, secrets to learn,
and places to visit.

Carmen and Juni had to dodge the Fooglies— captured spies that Floop turned into monsters!

They used cool space-age gadgets, like talking
watches and blast-off backpacks. . . .

And battled
Floop's army
of thumb
thumbs and
robot children.

But their fight had just begun. If Carmen and Juni didn't rescue their parents and stop Floop from using his secret weapon, the world would be doomed!

"Felix told us to deliver a message to the OSS," Carmen said. "And I guess that's you. The message is: The Third Brain lives."

A huge smile came over Ms. Gradenko's face. "Are you sure? The Third Brain lives?" She looked really excited.

Carmen nodded.

"Carmen, congratulations. You have now joined the ranks of super women spies in the OSS," Ms. Gradenko announced. She took off her silver OSS bracelet and strapped it onto Carmen's wrist. "You're brilliant."

Cool! Carmen thought. She beamed proudly. Now, *this* was the kind of adventure she'd been dying to have!

"Where would this Third Brain live, exactly?" Ms. Gradenko asked. "Did Felix tell you that? Is it here?"

"I don't think he said," Carmen answered.

"Search the place," Ms. Gradenko ordered the men.

The agents began opening drawers and cabinets. They looked under the pillows and bed cushions. As they rummaged through everything, they knocked over a framed photo of Mr. and Mrs. Cortez that was standing on a cabinet.

Juni reached over to set the photograph back up. He didn't notice that below the picture was a secret compartment. And in that compartment was—the Third Brain!

The small artificial brain was only the size of a jumbo egg, but it looked amazing. Parts of it were slightly pinkish gray, like a real brain. The other parts were shiny silver and electronic.

The photograph flipped over again. This time, the brain was in full view of everyone in the room, suspended from a wire frame. But no one noticed.

Juni went to the window and looked through it. There were more agents out there. He couldn't believe what they were doing. They had blasted apart the door to the Super Guppy and let water inside! They had made it sink!

Suddenly, Ms. Gradenko spotted the brain. "Oh, my!" she gasped, walking toward it. "It's so incredibly beautiful."

"Stop her!" Juni cried to Carmen. "They're working for Floop!"

But it was too late.

Ms. Gradenko had already put on a cotton glove and gently lifted the brain from the wire crown. Then she whirled around with a hard look in her eyes.

"Fly this to Floop's castle immediately!" she told all the agents. She handed the brain to one of them.

Carmen's mouth dropped open as the truth sank in.

Ms. Gradenko had lied to them! She wasn't on Mom and Dad's side at all!

She was working for Floop!

CHAPTERTWELVE

Carmen grabbed one of the spy gadgets she and Juni had found in the safe house. She pointed it at Ms. Gradenko and the men.

"Don't move," Carmen warned.

Everyone froze for an instant. Then Ms. Gradenko burst out laughing. So did the other agents. "Do you even know what those things are?" she asked with a mocking laugh.

Carmen glanced at the gadget in her hand. Juni was holding one too.

Uh-oh. These weren't weapons?

"Well, I know they're heavy!" Carmen said. Then she and Juni both threw the spy gadgets at Ms. Gradenko as hard as they could.

Ms. Gradenko ducked, and the gadgets hit the walls. The equipment smashed into tiny pieces.

Then the agent who was holding the Third Brain spotted the kids' backpacks. He strapped one onto his back and flipped a switch on the side. Instantly, he blasted out of the safe house, through an escape tunnel. The backpacks were *jet* packs!

Now I know why Mom and Dad were always training us! Carmen thought. Making us work out on the ropes and climbing equipment in our house. Teaching us to do gymnastics tumbles and karate leaps.

They were getting us ready for a time like this!

Carmen leaped through the air, jumping over one of the agents and landing on the countertop. Then she flipped over the ceiling fan, tumbling to the exact spot where the safe house jet packs were lined up on the floor.

She strapped one onto her back and flipped the on switch.

"Whoa!" Carmen cried as she felt the force of the jets. The pack blasted her out of the safe house, through the same escape tunnel.

"Wait for me!" Juni cried.

I can't, Carmen thought. She couldn't stop. Besides, she had to catch up with that guy and get the brain back!

The jet pack zoomed her through the tunnel. Then Carmen flew up into the air through a sky-light.

As soon as she was outside, she realized they were flying over the choppy, blue water. The agent who had escaped ahead of her was speeding away toward the shore.

There must be some way to control this thing, Carmen thought. She pressed a button on the jet pack. It went faster!

Yes! Carmen congratulated herself. She was already catching up with him.

There was only one problem. The guy with the brain was zooming straight toward a huge billboard onshore. On the billboard was a giant ad for Floop's Fooglies.

If she didn't veer away soon, she'd crash.

"You're not getting away with this, mister," Carmen muttered. Quickly, she powered forward, sneaking up on the agent. She took him by surprise, swooping up under him and grabbing for the brain in his hands. She pulled. Hard.

The agent struggled. He pushed on Carmen's face and tried to kick her out of the way. But Carmen was tough. Her parents had trained her to be strong. She didn't give up. She held on tight and finally yanked the small brain out of his hands.

Then she shot straight up in the air—an instant before, she would have smacked into the billboard.

"Phew!" Carmen said with a sigh of relief. Her heart hammered as she waited to see if the agent would follow her. But he didn't. While they were fighting, he hadn't noticed the billboard, so he didn't turn away in time. He crashed right through it, leaving a large hole.

A moment later, five more agents crashed through behind him!

Wow, Carmen thought. All those guys were following me!

At least now she was safe. And she had the
brain! But what had happened to Juni?

CHAPTERTHIRTEEN

Back in the safe house, Juni could hear his heart thumping in fear. His hands broke out in a sweat, and he felt his warts getting bigger and bumpier.

"Carmen!" Juni shouted into his communicator watch. "Don't leave me!"

He hoped that his sister was wearing her spy earpiece. But she didn't answer.

A moment later, the windows in the safe house all shattered. Then huge, muscular men dressed in black jumped through the broken glass. They wore black hoods over their thick, overgrown heads— just like the guys who had attacked Felix.

"I'm toast," Juni muttered.

Ms. Gradenko walked toward Juni with a large needle in her hands. She was smiling. "You know those shots you get at the doctor's office?" she said to Juni. "Well, don't worry. This hurts only a *little* bit more than those."

No! Juni thought wildly. He raced toward the jet packs that were lined up on the floor. But before he could reach them, the black-hooded muscle guys grabbed all the jet packs away.

All except one.

"That's mine!" Juni cried, lunging for it.

Two of the thugs tried to stop him. But Juni thought fast. He still had the silver metal lunch box handcuffed to his wrist. He swung it at the men, smacking them hard in the head. The lunch box knocked them both out—and popped off the handcuff at the same time.

Yes! Juni thought triumphantly as the hooded guys fell to the floor.

"Sleepy time," Ms. Gradenko said, coming at Juni with the needle.

"No!" Juni cried. He pounced on the one remaining jet pack, hoping to grab it and strap it on. But his hands failed him again, and he missed. Instead of grabbing the jet pack, he pounded the on switch. The jet pack zoomed across the room all by itself, straight for Ms. Gradenko. It exploded right beside her.

"Whoa!" Juni cried. The evil agent's hair had caught fire!

Quickly, one of the other agents doused out the flames with a bottle of soda water. Still, Ms. Gradenko's hair had burned to a horrible crisp. Most of it fell off. Only a few ugly strands remained on her bald scalp.

But Ms. Gradenko hardly seemed to notice. She marched toward Juni with the needle in her hands.

"You're not going anywhere," she told him.

Juni glanced around.

He was trapped. "Carmen! Save me!" he cried.

CHAPTERFOURTEEN

Carmen heard her brother's cry for help in her earpiece.

"Hang on, Juni," she told him as she swooped back toward the safe house. The small pink-and-silver brain was clasped tightly in her hands. She flipped the switch higher on her jet pack to pick up speed.

"I wonder if these things ever run out of gas," Carmen muttered.

She spotted Juni as soon as she reached the safe house escape tunnel. Ms. Gradenko was just about to inject him with some sick-looking green liquid.

"Juni! Run!" Carmen shouted.

She shot forward through the tunnel and grabbed her brother. With the power of the jet pack, she was able to yank him away from Ms. Gradenko. Then she steered toward the skylight, with Juni hanging on for dear life.

"D-don't ever leave me alone again!" Juni said, clutching the jet pack. Then, to his horror, his fingers began to slip.

"Hang on, Butterfingers!" Carmen shouted.

Together, they shot up into the sky. Once again, Carmen looked down at the ocean surrounding the safe house. Then she headed straight for the coastline in the distance. Time to rescue Mom and Dad!

A few minutes later, she and Juni were sitting on a park bench in some coastal city. Carmen glanced around, trying to figure out exactly where they were. It was definitely near home. But she wasn't sure which city. The only thing she knew was that she and Juni were safe.

"Wow," Juni said. "That was intense."

"I know," Carmen agreed. "But at least I've got the brain." She took it out of her pocket and handed it to him.

Juni turned the tiny brain over in his hands. He stared at it, thinking.

"You know what?" he said finally. "We should destroy this. I think that's what Mom and Dad would want us to do."

"Are you nuts?" Carmen tried to grab the brain away from her brother. "That's our bargaining chip for getting Mom and Dad back!"

"I know," Juni said. "But it's what Floop wants. Mom and Dad wouldn't want him to have it. I think it should be destroyed."

"You're wrong. Until this morning, we didn't

even know Mom and Dad were spies!" Carmen pointed out. "So there's no way you can know what they'd want us to do. We keep the brain—for now."

"But what about the spy book?" Juni argued. "A good spy thinks like his enemy, remember?"

Carmen sighed. "Leave the Third Brain alone, Juni. And give your own brain a rest."

Juni frowned. But maybe his big sister was right. How could they be sure what their parents would want?

Suddenly, Juni noticed the OSS bracelet she was wearing.

"Hey, why are you still wearing that thing?" he asked. "Those agents could be tracking us with it. Did you ever think of that?"

"Oh, right," Carmen said, rolling her eyes. She stood up and marched away to a drinking fountain. When her little brother wasn't looking, she slipped the bracelet off. Then she turned it over, just to prove to herself that it was only a piece of jewelry.

Carmen froze. The back of the bracelet was blinking!

"Oh, no!" she cried. Juni was right!

"I hate that," she muttered to herself. Then she glanced around nervously. Had someone already followed them?

She checked over her shoulder, half expecting to see Ms. Gradenko. Or more agents. Or those weird guys dressed in black hoods.

But she didn't see anyone else in the park.

Just kids on the playground.

So far, so good. Carmen sighed.

But she and Juni had to get out of there. And fast—while they still had a chance!

CHAPTERFIFTEEN

Floop paced in his castle. He was trying to record a new song for his TV show.

"'I'm just a little elephant,'" Floop sang. "'Don't want to be the monster. I want to run around. I'm just a little elephant. Don't want to play with lightning. . . .'"

The song was crazy. It didn't make any sense. Like most of Floop's ideas, it was twisted and demented and strange. But he was trying to make sense out of it.

"'I just want to say hello,'" he sang. "'And when no one's around, I'll just stay mellow . . . .'"

No good. Floop waved his arms at the camera.

"*Cut!*" he shouted angrily. "Stop the tape! It's not working! Not working!" He turned and motioned toward the Fooglies behind him. "Lock them up!" Floop ordered the Thumb Thumbs.

Then he stomped out of the TV studio and

marched into the control room. Minion was waiting for him.

"My show is a mess," Floop moaned. "What does it need, Minion?"

"I don't know what you mean, sir," Minion answered.

"My show. It *needs* something. Something that will take it to number one in the ratings." Floop shook his head. "I can *feel* it, Minion. Something's missing. But I can't figure out what it is."

"Maybe you're spending too much time on this program," Minion said. "You should be more concerned with our evil, diabolical plans."

"Plans? Huh? What plans?" Floop looked distracted.

"The army of robot children, sir!" Minion reminded him.

"Oh. Those plans. I don't know," Floop said. He sounded tired. "How can we succeed if we don't have those two Cortez children? They escaped from the safe house, didn't they?"

Minion looked down at the floor. "Yes. And not only did they escape—they took the Third Brain with them!"

Floop's head whipped around, and his eyes sparked to life. "It exists?" he asked.

Minion nodded. "Completely. Gregorio Cortez lied to us. He didn't destroy it."

"Excellent!" Floop clapped his hands. "Send out our best Thumbs to get it. I want that brain!"

"Sir?" Minion began. "May I make a small suggestion? If you want to catch a criminal, you send a criminal. But if you want to snare a spy, you send a spy."

Floop scowled. "Oh, for heaven's sake, speak English!" he snapped. "My brain is fried! I've been baking under studio lights all day!"

"All I'm saying is, if you want to find a child, send a child," Minion explained patiently.

Floop's eyes lit up. "You mean, send the Spy Kids? My robots? That's brilliant, Minion!"

"Thank you, sir," Minion said. "I thought so too. They're already on their way."

CHAPTERSIXTEEN

Carmen quickly tossed the OSS bracelet into a nearby trash can. Then she bent down to take a drink of water. She didn't want Juni to suspect there was anything wrong. Or that he'd been right about the tracer.

We'd better get out of here—pronto! Carmen thought. Before someone finds us.

She glanced up from the water fountain. Juni was standing right in front of her. He just stared at her without blinking.

Carmen narrowed her eyes. "What are you wearing?" she asked, glancing at him up and down.

Juni had changed his clothes. But why? Carmen wondered. And how?

Her brother was dressed in a strange gray outfit with straight-legged pants and a pullover top. It looked like something a Martian would wear in a space-age hospital operating room.

Juni still didn't speak. He just stared silently.

"What's wrong with you?" Carmen asked, frowning. "Say something."

"Gib, jub gub-gub glee," Juni said. "Wub wub mucky-mucky, hig wag bug-dug wob. Blehhh."

"You just get dumber by the minute," Carmen told him.

She whirled away, then stopped short.

Across the park, she saw another Juni! And that one was talking to someone who looked just like *her*!

Uh-oh, Carmen thought, her throat closing up. There are *two* of us! Two Junis and two Carmens!

Carmen's mind raced, trying to figure it out. That one across the park must be the *real* Juni, she decided. Because he's wearing his normal clothes.

She turned back around and stared at the fake Juni behind her. The one in the spacey gray outfit. Suddenly, his eyes flickered. A bright red electronic light was glowing inside them.

He's a robot! Carmen realized instantly.

She formed her hand into a fist. "I've always wanted to do this," she said.

She pulled back and punched the robot in the face. Hard.

"Ow!" Carmen cried as her fist hit the robot's rock-solid face.

She smacked it again, even harder this time, but the robot still didn't react.

Okay, forget it! Carmen decided. She turned to

run, but the Juni robot grabbed her. He was strong. Much stronger than she was.

"Juni!" Carmen called to her real brother. "You were right! Destroy the brain!"

Juni heard her and looked over. He tried to do what Carmen said. But the Carmen robot picked Juni up and tossed him onto a merry-go-round in the playground. Then she spun the merry-go-round so fast, he couldn't get off.

While it was spinning, the robot hopped on and tore the Third Brain out of Juni's grasp. He tried to stop her, but the fake Carmen overpowered him.

All Juni could do was reach up and grab the ID tag that hung on a chain around her neck.

"Carmen! Help!" he cried to his real sister. Why wasn't she ever there when he needed her?

With the brain in her hands, the Carmen robot jumped off the merry-go-round and joined her electronic brother. Then the two of them blasted off into space, propelled by jets in their shoes.

A bunch of kids on the playground watched in awe.

"Hey, I want shoes like that! They're cool!" one of them shouted.

Carmen raced over to see if Juni was all right.

"Did they take the brain?" she asked anxiously.

Juni nodded. "But I got her necklace," he said. He showed Carmen the ID tag.

She read it carefully. It said: *Floop Industries. Limited Edition SPY KID. One of 500.*

"One of five hundred?" Carmen said. "Oh, wow. That means Floop's going to have tons of those things flying around! They'll be everywhere!"

"I think the brain's going to make them smart," Juni said.

Carmen eyed her brother sideways. Juni was probably right, she decided. Again.

"If the robots all get brains like that one, they'll be unstoppable," Juni said softly.

"I know," Carmen agreed. Her throat got that tight, worried feeling again.

What if we don't find Floop before he puts brains in the robots? she thought. What if . . .

Don't think that way, she told herself.

"Come on, Juni. We have to get to Floop—now!" she said. "Before five hundred robots get a lot smarter—and Mom and Dad get their faces erased!"

CHAPTERSEVENTEEN

"Where are we?" Juni asked Carmen, look-ing around. The two of them had just climbed out of a taxicab.

Carmen paid the driver and pointed toward a low building across the street. "Machete's Spy Shop," she answered. "See? That's the name that was on all that spy stuff we found."

"And the name of the best man at Mom and Dad's wedding?" Juni asked, remembering.

Carmen nodded, and grabbed Juni's hand as they crossed the street. For once, she didn't mind holding on to her brother. It felt much safer that way.

Two Cortezes are better than one, she thought.

Carmen marched into Machete's workshop with-out knocking.

A gruff-looking man with long hair and a pock-marked face sat at a workbench. He held a hot, pointed electric tool in one hand. He was using it to melt something on the index finger of his other hand.

"Is *that* Machete?" Juni whispered.

"It must be," Carmen answered. "There's no one else here."

Juni cleared his throat and got up the nerve to speak. "What are you working on?" he asked the man.

"The world's smallest camera," the man answered. He wiggled his index finger at Juni.

"I don't see it," Juni said.

"No. But it sees you," the man said with a laugh. He nodded toward a TV monitor above his head. The tiny camera on the man's finger was taping Juni and Carmen right then! They could see themselves on the TV.

"You're Machete? And you sell spy stuff here?" Carmen asked.

The man laughed again. "Come back with your parents," he said.

"We can't," Carmen said in a serious voice.

Machete put down his tools and eyed them more closely. "Who are you?"

"Carmen Elizabeth Juanita Echo Sky Brava Cortez," Carmen answered.

Instantly, a locked door in the back of Machete's shop opened—all by itself.

Wow! Carmen thought. My name works in all kinds of places!

Machete's eyes widened. "So you're. . . ?" he started to ask.

Carmen nodded. "Gregorio Cortez is our father. You were his best man."

"Hmmph." Machete crossed his arms over his chest. "You two will turn around and leave my shop immediately," he said coldly. "I don't ever want to hear my brother's name again."

Brother? Carmen shot a questioning glance at Juni. Their dad had a brother? That was news to them.

"You're our *uncle?*" she asked, amazed.

Machete nodded. "Gregorio is my younger brother."

"Wow. So you're a secret agent too?" Carmen said.

"Not exactly," Machete said. "But I create the best spy inventions in the world."

Carmen glanced around the shop again. She noticed a pair of spy glasses just like the ones Ms. Gradenko's men wore.

"You sell your spy inventions to both sides, don't you?" Carmen guessed.

"Correct." Machete shrugged. "Why shouldn't I?"

"Why shouldn't you? Because the bad guys do bad things with them!" Juni answered, shocked.

"So that's why Dad hasn't told us about you," Carmen said slowly. "Because you don't care which side you're on."

Machete frowned. "I don't see the difference," he said.

"Well, we do," Carmen shot back.

"Did you ever sell stuff to Floop?" Juni asked.

"Why do you ask?" Machete said, turning back to his work.

"Because our mom and dad—your *brother*—are Floop's prisoners right now," Carmen told him. "And if we don't help them, something really bad's going to happen."

Machete turned around again. Carmen could tell he was trying to stay tough, but inside he really cared. At least she hoped so.

"Gregorio's being held prisoner?" Machete asked.

Carmen nodded. "That's right. Is there any way you can help us get to Floop's castle? We need to go right away. Do you know where it is?"

Machete was quiet for a long time. He gazed out the window, thinking. Then he stood up and silently led them up a flight of stairs to the roof of his building.

"This is the only way," Machete said finally. He opened a huge door. Behind it was an amazingly small aircraft.

He pulled the jet plane out of its hangar.

"Cool!" Juni muttered under his breath. "But it's so tiny."

"It's built for only one passenger," Machete said. "But it's fast."

"One *adult* passenger," Carmen said with a smile. "It could fit two small kids. And Juni is definitely a shrimp."

"Am not," Juni said.

Machete reached inside the aircraft and pushed a few buttons. "This baby almost flies itself," he bragged. "I can program your destination. . . . " He entered the numbers that corresponded to the location of Floop's castle. "And I can set the autopilot. It should fly right there, but you'll have to take over if something goes wrong."

Carmen and Juni exchanged a quick glance. Was their uncle saying he'd let them fly the plane? That would be awesome!

"So, will you let us go ourselves?" Carmen asked excitedly.

"No!" Machete roared. "Of course not! This is not a toy!"

"Well, will you go yourself, then?" she begged.

"For your brother?" Juni pleaded.

Machete thought about it. He was silent for a long time. "No," he said finally.

Carmen's heart sank. Why was he being so hard-nosed? Her father could be like that too.

"Then how about for *us*?" she tried. "For your poor little niece and nephew—who will be orphans if we don't get our parents back."

"Please?" Juni begged.

"No," he said finally.

Then Machete turned and went back into his

shop. It sounded like Machete would never change his mind.

Ever.

CHAPTER EIGHTEEN

"**S**ir, you aren't paying attention," Minion said. "Look! They're perfect!"

Floop sat glumly in a giant chair shaped like a hand.

"Look at what?" he asked in a dull voice.

"At your Spy Kids!" Minion answered. "We have the president's daughter. And the prime minister's son, the general's daughter, copies of all the richest people's children. They're all here, as planned."

"But do we have the real children? The Cortez children?" Floop asked.

"No," Minion admitted. "But we don't need them now."

Floop didn't seem to be listening. His mind was somewhere else. "I have to get back to my show," he said, climbing out of the giant chair. He walked slowly through the Grand Room, past all the crazy colorful furniture.

"Focus on the task at hand, sir," Minion called after him. "Mr. Lisp is coming back today. We have only until noon to prepare a demonstration for him."

Floop stopped and looked Minion straight in the eye. "I don't believe in this project anymore, Minion," Floop said. "I don't think I ever did."

"Excuse me?" Minion said.

"The mutated agents and the robot kids? What good are they? Those weren't *my* ideas. They're *yours*," Floop said.

"So?" Minion said.

"I think that's why they're not working," Floop said.

"Not yet, they don't," Minion said.

He snapped his fingers, and two more robots marched into the room. They were the Carmen and Juni robots. They handed Minion the Third Brain.

"But you see," Minion went on, holding up the small brain, "they'll all be working very soon. I don't need you anymore, Floop."

As if on command, the Carmen and Juni Spy Kids marched toward Floop and grabbed his arms, taking him prisoner.

Floop's face filled with disappointment. "Minion!" he said. "How could you?"

Minion took off his thick black glasses and tossed them aside. He glared at Floop triumphantly. "I assure you, it will be *Mister* Minion from now on. And you, Floop, have served your purpose.

Children, lock him in the Virtual Room!"

"The Virtual Room?" Floop repeated. "But . . . there's no way out of there."

"I know." Minion smiled with evil as the robot children dragged Floop away.

As soon as his former boss was gone, Minion marched through the large castle to the Transmogrification Room. That was where all the equipment that could transform secret agents into Fooglies was kept.

Now comes the fun part, Minion thought. He rubbed his hands together in delight.

In one part of the room, Mr. Cortez was strapped into the transmogrification chair. His wife was tied up nearby.

"Well," Mr. Cortez said as Minion entered. "If it isn't Alexander Minion."

"Agent Cortez," Minion greeted him with a nod. "Wonderful to see you again—after all these years."

Mrs. Cortez's head snapped toward her husband. "You *know* him?" she asked, surprised.

Her husband looked embarrassed about hiding things from her. "Well, yes," he admitted. "There was a time when he was one of our best agents." He looked back at Minion. "So, where is Floop?"

"I've taken care of him. He's in . . . a dream state," Minion answered.

Mr. Cortez shook his head. "A double cross, huh? Your specialty."

"Thank you," Minion answered proudly.

Mr. Cortez sneaked a glance at his wife. From her face, he knew what she was thinking. She was terribly worried about their children—about what Minion might do to them.

What if he had already taken them prisoner? And what if Minion threatened to hurt the kids unless their dad helped him with the Third Brain?

"I'm *not* going to help you, Minion," Mr. Cortez said.

Minion just smirked and pointed to the Third Brain. "I don't need your help anymore," he declared gleefully. "I finally have what I wanted. To be honest, I should probably just go on with my business. But I'm in the mood for a little revenge."

"What's he talking about?" Mrs. Cortez asked her husband.

Mr. Cortez slumped in the transmogrification chair. Quickly, he explained the whole story to her. Minion had worked with him on the Ten Brains project—for a while. Then he had realized that Minion was trying to ruin the whole thing. Insert his own ideas. Take all the power.

So Mr. Cortez turned him in—and Minion was kicked out of the OSS.

"So that's why he wants to hurt us?" Mrs. Cortez asked.

Her husband nodded.

Minion picked up Floop's ball of clay—the clay he used to create the Fooglies.

"I must apologize. I'm not nearly the artist Floop

is," Minion said with an evil laugh. "But don't worry. I've got something special in mind for you."

He pulled a drawing out of his pocket. It was the hideous Fooglie Juni had created. The creature had a giant, lumpy bald head, and weird eyes floating all over it.

"No!" Mrs. Cortez gasped under her breath.

But there was nothing she or her husband could do. Minion quickly shaped the lump of clay to match the Fooglie drawing. Then he pushed the button.

"Ahhh!" Mr. Cortez cried as electronic waves shot through him.

In seconds, the transmogrification machine had turned Carmen and Juni's dad into a creepy, sickening Fooglie!

CHAPTERNINETEEN

"Do you think we can make it?" Juni whispered to his sister later that night.

The two of them stood on the roof of Machete's shop. A full moon shone in the clear, dark sky. Machete was asleep in his bed, below.

"I've flown this thing a zillion times," Carmen said, gazing at the small jet plane's complicated controls.

"Yeah, right," Juni said. "The *game* version."

"So?" Carmen said. "The controls are all the same. And Machete programmed it, remember? Come on. Let's go!"

She climbed into the tiny spy plane. Juni followed, pulling the clear plastic cover over their heads.

With the touch of one button, the jet lifted off the roof and swooped into the night sky at a crazy speed.

"Whoa!" Juni cried, half scared, half excited. "It's totally fast!"

"Yeah," Carmen said, swallowing hard. "And I'm not even doing anything!"

They zoomed through the sky, past tall buildings, over low houses, and out across the water toward . . . somewhere. Toward Floop's castle, hopefully.

"There's only one thing I never learned to do in the game," Carmen said.

"What's that?" Juni asked.

"Land." Carmen felt a little sick to her stomach.

Juni shrugged. "How hard can it be?" he asked.

Before his sister could answer, the jet started to rock back and forth wildly.

"Uh-oh," Carmen said. She quickly checked out all the instruments on the panel. "Something's wrong."

"Well, figure it out!" Juni said anxiously. "Fast!"

Carmen stared at the instruments again. Airspeed—okay. Altitude—okay. Autopilot . . .

"Yikes!" she said. "Autopilot *failing*! We're going to have to fly this thing ourselves! Just like Machete said. Take the controls. I'll switch it to manual!"

Juni grabbed the joystick and steered the plane. It was just like the RX Flight Simulator video game.

The plane stopped rocking. But now they were headed straight for a mountain peak!

"What are you doing?" Carmen cried. "Pull the plane up—or we're going to crash!"

Juni yanked on the joystick. The plane veered off to the right. But the tip of one wing clipped the mountaintop and ripped off.

The plane immediately dipped sideways and began to fall toward the ground.

"Now you've done it!" Carmen shouted at her brother angrily. "We're going to crash now for sure!"

"No, we're not," Juni yelled.

Thinking fast, he pulled up on the joystick. Then he guided the plane toward another mountain peak. This time, the mountain was on the left.

Carmen closed her eyes when she realized what her brother was doing.

Ka-rash! The left wing tip ripped off just like the right one had.

"You did that on purpose!" Carmen screamed in disbelief.

"Yeah," Juni said, feeling very proud of himself. "Now it's balanced."

Balanced? Carmen sighed. Her little brother was right. Again. I *hate* that, she thought.

But at least the plane wasn't rocking anymore.

A few moments later, Carmen and Juni spotted Floop's castle in the distance. It rose straight up from the small craggy island in the middle of the ocean, just like on the TV show.

Carmen reached out and pushed the landing gear button. It flashed red.

"There is no landing gear!" Juni cried. "I think I

knocked it off accidentally when we passed that last mountain!"

Okay, Carmen thought. No problem. I can handle this.

She tried to stay cool, but her heart was pounding furiously.

What would Mom do at a time like this? she wondered.

She reached out and pushed another button on the control panel. This one said Drop.

Maybe that will make the plane drop, Carmen thought.

But she was wrong. Instantly, the floor opened beneath them. She and Juni fell out of the plane—and plunged straight toward the cold shark-filled waters!

CHAPTER TWENTY

"**A**re you all right?" Carmen called to her brother.

Slowly, Juni pulled himself to the water's edge and climbed out onto a stone platform. He wiped the water from his eyes and looked around.

"W-where are we?" he asked, shivering from the cold.

Carmen gazed around at the stone enclosure they were in. It looked a lot like a cave, with stone floors and walls lined with flaming torches.

"In Floop's castle," she guessed. "Probably in the dungeon. The dungeon must open into the ocean."

She pulled herself out of the water beside Juni and sighed with relief. "Well, at least we survived," she said. "I can't believe we actually swam through all those sharks. But—" She stopped when she heard the noise.

It was one of Floop's Thumb Thumbs, marching toward them.

Juni gasped when he saw the hulking creature.

Carmen quickly reached into her pocket and pulled out her newest secret weapon—a gumball. She stuck it in her mouth, chewed it up, and spat it at the creepy thumb-headed thing.

The gumball stuck to the Thumb Thumb's neck—just below the thumbnail. Then it exploded with a *zap!*

The big thumb hit the floor. Hard.

"What did you *do* to him?" Juni asked.

Carmen handed her brother a few of the gumballs. They were individually wrapped. "Machete's Electro Shock Gumballs," she explained. "I took them from Uncle Machete's shop before we left."

"Cool," Juni said, pocketing the candy. "Now what?"

"Now we find Mom and Dad," Carmen announced. She pulled Juni through the open door leading into the castle.

The two of them tiptoed up a winding staircase to the level above. Everywhere they looked, there were odd and interesting things. Along the walls, Floop had placed strange drawings and sculptures. All the furniture looked like toys. And some of the doors were optical illusions.

The first room they passed was labeled Virtual Room.

"What's in there?" Carmen asked her brother.

"That's where all the digital sets are created for Floop's TV show," Juni explained.

"A perfect place to hide," Carmen muttered. "Maybe Mom and Dad are in there."

She reached for the doorknob.

Juni stopped her. "No way," he said. "It's a perfect place to get lost! Once you go in there, nothing is real. It's filled with computer images. You won't know where the door is or anything! It's the *worst* place you could go."

"Okay," Carmen said. "We'll keep looking."

She and Juni headed toward a long hallway that curved toward the Grand Room. But as they got closer, they heard footsteps. Marching footsteps.

Both kids jumped back, out of sight.

"Who is it?" Juni whispered, trying to see around his sister.

"It's more of those robots—the Spy Kids," Carmen said softly. "A whole army of them!"

The Spy Kids marched past Carmen and Juni without even blinking. They didn't seem to see them.

"Come on," Carmen said. "We'll just get in line behind them. No one will notice us there."

She and Juni joined the back of the line. They marched side by side, just like the robots, two at a time.

But just as they neared the Grand Room of the castle, the Spy Kids suddenly turned on them.

"Intruder!" the robot nearest them announced.

The next one down the line repeated the word. "Intruder!" And then the next one.

Pretty soon, all the Spy Kid robots were saying it. "Intruder!" they called, staring at Juni and Carmen. "Intruder!"

Uh-oh, Carmen thought. The Spy Kids have definitely gotten a lot smarter since the last time we saw them!

"Run!" Carmen ordered her brother. Then she took off down another mazelike hall.

"Wait for me!" Juni cried, following her.

They both ran as fast as they could, trying to escape the powerfully strong robot kids. Carmen skidded around a corner—and slid to the edge of a huge, gaping pit in the floor. The Spy Kids were right behind her.

"We'll have to jump!" Carmen called to Juni.

She took a few steps back, then ran forward as fast as she could.

But her leap wasn't powerful enough. She missed.

"NO!" Juni cried as his sister fell into the deep, dark hole. "Don't leave me!"

"Juniiiiiiiiii!"

It was the last thing Carmen said.

The floor closed, sealing the pit. Now Juni was totally alone.

CHAPTERTWENTY-ONE

Juni's heart pounded. He wasn't sure which was louder—his heartbeat or the sounds of the Spy Kids marching down the halls.

They were coming to get him.

I've got to hide, he told himself. But where?

He rounded a corner and saw that he was right back where they started: in front of the Virtual Room.

Clomp, clomp, clomp! The robots were drawing nearer.

Juni's hands itched like crazy. He scratched them and noticed that his nervous warts were getting bigger. Much bigger.

Open the door and face your fear, he thought. Dad told me that the other day.

Okay, Juni decided. Maybe now was the time.

He opened the door to the Virtual Room, and ducked inside.

"Whoa!" Juni gasped in awe.

The room was a blur of different worlds. Skies. Landscapes. Clouds. Rainbows. But right smack in the middle was the biggest image of all.

A giant Floop!

"Floop!" Juni cried, gawking up at the two-hundred-foot-tall image of his TV hero.

"Welcome to loneliness," Floop said sadly.

He was lying on his back in the clouds, as if he were trapped there. Then he held up his hand, the one with the weird black glove on it. He pointed one of the fingers at Juni. The finger had a face!

"You there," Floop said, using his finger like a puppet and making it talk. "What's that on your hands?"

"Nothing," Juni lied, hiding his hands behind his back.

"They're warts, aren't they?" Floop said. "From being scared all the time. Right?"

Juni nodded.

"I used to be scared when I was your age," Floop said. "I was afraid I'd never be good at anything. Never do anything special. But I found that if I gave my fears a personality, then I could understand them. See?"

Not really, Juni thought. Floop wasn't making a lot of sense. And besides, he was just a big bully!

He scowled at the giant Floop.

"You don't look very scared to me," Floop said.

"That's because I'm mad," Juni said. "I thought

you were a genius. Someone creative and artistic."

Floop's mouth turned up in a small smile. "You did?" he asked. "That's what I wanted to be."

"But you're not!" Juni said. "You're just mean and greedy! You kidnapped my parents, made psycho robot children, and swallowed up my sister!"

"But I don't want to be like that anymore," Floop said. "Honestly. I don't know how that happened."

Juni saw a tear form in the corner of the giant man's eye. "Well, why don't you leave, then?" Juni asked, crossing his arms. "You can stop those robots."

"No, I can't," Floop said. "I'm a prisoner in here. Once you enter the Virtual Room, there's no way out—unless someone turns the program off."

Juni glanced down at his hands again. They were sweating, and two more warts had popped out.

"You . . . you watch my show?" Floop asked hopefully.

"I used to," Juni said.

Floop sighed. "I've never met any of my viewers before. Honestly, I know you're disappointed in me. And you have every right to be. But I never meant for any of this to happen. I let people lead me in the wrong direction. All this evil business was Minion's idea. I just wanted to have fun."

"Really?" Juni wanted to believe the Fabulous Floop. But he wasn't sure he should trust him. "So Minion is really the evil one?"

Floop nodded.

"What would you do if you could shut down this Virtual Room and get out of here?" Juni asked.

"Impossible," Floop replied. "It can be turned off only from outside."

"But just suppose," Juni urged.

"Well, first I'd stop Minion," Floop declared. "Stop the robot army. Reverse all the transformations. Try to reclaim my own soul. And hope the world would forgive me."

"Is that the truth?" Juni asked.

"Yes," Floop said. "But like I said, it's no use."

"I'm not so sure about that," Juni said. "I have an idea. And I think it might work!"

CHAPTERTWENTY-TWO

Juni reached into his pocket—and pulled out five Machete's Electro Shock Gumballs. He popped one into his mouth and started chewing.

"What's that?" the giant Floop asked from his cloud.

"My secret weapon," Juni said, chewing hard. "Minion must be stopped. And I want my family back."

He popped another gumball in. Then another. Pretty soon he was chewing all five exploding gumballs.

"Okay, kid," Floop said. "I hope your plan will work—whatever it is. But let me ask you just one question first. My show. What does it need? It's missing *something,* but I can't figure out what."

Floop's show? Juni thought for a minute. It had always been his favorite. But he supposed it could be better.

"Kids," Juni answered finally, his mouth full of gum. "It needs kids."

"You're right!" Floop said, sitting up taller. His face glowed. "Kids! What a wonderful idea!"

"Hold still," Juni instructed him.

The gum in his mouth felt ready. He took it out and hurled it at the giant image of Floop.

Ka-bam! There was an amazing explosion as the gum hit the virtual Floop right between the eyes!

Then the whole room lit up. The colorful images flickered on and off. Then they disappeared.

"You did it!" Floop cried.

Juni blinked, trying to figure out where he was. All the computerized skies and mountains and clouds were gone. So was the huge Floop. All that remained was a simple round room with green and blue panels on the walls.

And a door. He could see the door!

The real Floop lay on the floor in front of Juni. He jumped to his feet. "I'm myself again!" he cried. "Thank you, thank you!"

"No problem," Juni replied. "But we've still got work to do. It's time to stop Minion."

Together, Juni and Floop ran out of the Virtual Room and into the hallway. Two Thumb Thumbs charged at them—one at Juni, the other at Floop.

"Go to the dungeon! Let my parents out!" Juni called to Floop. "I'll take care of this guy!"

Floop stuck out his foot and tripped one of the Thumb Thumbs. Then he darted down a staircase.

Juni struck a karate pose and got ready for the other Thumb. He spun around fast and kicked the big ugly thing in the head. "That's for my sister!" he shouted, knocking the freak to the ground.

But as it fell, the Thumb's "head" fell off. It was just a costume! And there was a person inside!

"Ouch," the person said, holding her head.

"Carmen!" Juni cried, happy to see his sister again. "How did you escape?"

"I don't know," Carmen answered. "I found a secret passageway, and this Thumb Thumb costume, so I put it on as a disguise. But watch out for the other Thumbs—they're real."

"Come on," Juni said, heading toward the staircase Floop had used. "We've got to find Mom and Dad!"

Carmen struggled to get out of the oversize costume. Then she followed her brother down the stone steps. The hallway curved around, past a whole bunch of cells.

"Mom? Where are you?" Carmen called, racing along.

"Carmen? Juni?" their mother answered.

Carmen ran to the end of the hall. Her mother was being held in the last cell. Floop was already there, unlocking it.

"But where's Dad?" Carmen asked.

Before her mother could answer, a large purple arm shot out from the neighboring cell.

Carmen gasped, recognizing the Fooglie inside.

It was the same hideous being Juni had drawn! The ugly thing with eyes floating all over its disgustingly knobby bald head!

But that wasn't the most horrible part. Carmen recognized the human being underneath.

"Dad?" she cried.

CHAPTERTWENTY-THREE

Carmen couldn't believe her eyes.

Was that really her father—trapped inside that hideous Fooglie body?

"Mom! What did they do to him?" Carmen cried.

Behind her, Juni gasped. "That's my Fooglie!" Juni said. "The one I drew!"

Mrs. Cortez stepped out of the cell and pulled her children close. "Don't worry, sweethearts," she said. "I'll . . . I'll think of something to save your father. But how did you two get here?"

"We used our wits," Carmen said, beaming. Then she turned and shot her little brother a genuine smile.

But Juni didn't notice. He was glaring at his former idol, Floop. "You turned my dad into a Fooglie?" Juni accused him.

"No. *I* didn't," Floop said. "Minion did. But I might be able to change him back."

"Great!" Juni cried. "Do it! Now! The rest of us will go take care of Minion. Come on, Mom!"

Wow, Carmen thought in admiration. What happened to *him*? He used to be such a wimp!

Carmen and her mother ran to catch up with Juni. He was already climbing the stairs to the Grand Room. The three Cortezes stood out of sight, peering in to eavesdrop on Minion.

As they watched, Mr. Lisp arrived. He sat in Floop's big throne, the one that was shaped like a hand. Except Mr. Lisp kept sliding off.

Minion paced back and forth in front of him.

"Mr. Lisp, your army will arrive any moment," Minion said. "I'm sorry to say that Floop cannot join us right now—he's not here. But I myself would be happy to form a partnership with you."

Juni's eyes lit up. "I have an idea," he whispered to his mom and sister. "Come with me."

Carmen and their mother looked puzzled, but they followed Juni to one of the TV control rooms. He picked up a microphone and flipped a few switches so that his voice would be heard on the speakers in the Grand Room.

Then he began to talk—in a perfect imitation of Floop's voice!

"Minion, this is Floop," Juni said. "Please report to the robotics lab at once! We have a huge, major, big-time problem!"

Carmen giggled as they watched Minion on a TV monitor.

"Look at him," Mrs. Cortez whispered. "He's totally freaked out!"

"He thinks Floop is still locked up in the Virtual Room," Juni explained to his mom. "He can't figure out how Floop can be talking to him."

Carmen flipped another switch on the control panel so they could listen to Minion and Mr. Lisp.

"I thought you said Floop wasn't here," Mr. Lisp accused Minion.

"Uh, he's not," Minion tried to explain. "Not *here* here. He's in the *castle*, just not in this room. See?"

Carmen giggled again.

"Lisp doesn't look too happy," Mrs. Cortez said.

"But he will be if he gets those Spy Kid robots!" Carmen said. "We'd better do something to stop them."

"Right," her mom agreed. The two of them hurried from the room.

Juni spoke into the microphone again. "Minion, I'm not kidding. We have a real-deal gigantic problem! A serious setback with the Spy Kids! Come to the Transmogrification Room immediately!"

Large beads of sweat appeared on Minion's forehead.

"Excuse me a moment," he said to Mr. Lisp. "I, uh, have to check on something. Something important. I'll be right back."

Then he stormed out of the room.

Juni ran through the large castle to the Transmogrification Room. He hoped he'd get there before Minion did. He also hoped desperately that Floop had been able to transform his father back to a normal human being.

But when Juni reached the room, it was empty. There was no way to know whether Floop had tried to save his father—or not.

Or whether Floop had failed.

Juni hid behind a door, waiting for Minion.

As soon as Minion entered the room, Juni spoke up from behind the door. Again, his voice was a perfect copy of Floop's.

"Minion!" Juni shouted.

"Where are you?" Minion asked. He whirled around, confused.

Juni wasn't sure what to say. He didn't want Minion to find him—alone—hiding behind the door.

He peered out through the crack by the door hinge.

"Dad!" Juni gasped softly.

His father was standing in the hallway, right behind Minion. Minion didn't see him.

There was a bit of steam rising from Mr. Cortez's head, but basically he looked okay. Floop had transformed him back to normal.

Juni's dad put a finger to his lips, warning Juni to stay quiet.

Then he lunged forward, taking Minion by surprise. He quickly pushed him onto the transformation chair and strapped him in.

Juni stepped out from behind the door.

"Cortez!" Minion whined. "Can't we make a deal?"

Juni mocked him perfectly. "Cortez! Can't we make a deal?" he said in Minion's voice. He was getting pretty good at doing imitations!

Minion's face fell. Suddenly, he realized it was all over. He was trapped.

"Clever boy you've got there, Cortez," Minion said. He didn't even try to fight anymore.

"I know," Juni's dad said with a proud smile. "He gets it from his mother."

"Dad, we've got to stop the Spy Kids!" Juni informed his father. "They've got brains now. And Mr. Lisp is here to take all of them away!"

"Right," Mr. Cortez said. "Let's go."

Quickly, he picked up the ball of clay that Floop used to mold the Fooglies. Then he smashed it into the weirdest being he could imagine, with three ugly heads.

"You'll be the weirdest Fooglie of all," Mr. Cortez told Minion.

"You can't possibly do it," Minion said. "You're too . . . too . . . nice."

"But *you* can do it," Mr. Cortez replied.

He handed the transmogrification button to Minion. Then he used Minion's thumb to press it down. He knew the transformation process would not start until Minion *released* the button.

"Don't let go now!" Mr. Cortez said as he and

Juni hurried out of the room.

Minion waited until they were gone. He gave a horrible, evil laugh.

"Fools!" he cried. Then he let go of the button— and let the transformation begin.

CHAPTER TWENTY-FOUR

"**H**ow did you kids get here?" Mr. Cortez asked his son as they hurried to find Floop.

"I flew a plane in," Juni said, talking fast. "On manual, Dad! But we had to destroy it in order to land."

"Huh?" His dad hadn't followed any of that.

"I'll tell you later," Juni said. "I'm just glad Floop changed you back into a human."

"He transformed Donnagon and Felix too. They're back to normal," Mr. Cortez said.

"Good," Juni said. "Come on—we've got to stop the Spy Kids!"

As they rounded a corner in the castle, they found Floop, Carmen, and Mrs. Cortez rushing to meet them.

"Bad news!" Floop announced. "The Spy Kids have already been programmed to do what Lisp wants. We've got to keep them from leaving the castle!"

"Programmed how?" Mr. Cortez asked.

"The Third Brain has been linked to all five hundred robots," Floop told him.

"Can't you just remove the brain?" Carmen asked.

Floop shook his head. "Minion *copied* the brain. He put one in each robot. We can't just take all five hundred brains out!"

"So don't," Carmen said. She'd suddenly had a great idea. "Change their programming!"

"That would take weeks," Floop said glumly.

Carmen's mind whirred, thinking fast. There had to be a way to stop those robots! "You don't have to rewrite the whole thing," she said. "Just two words."

Floop's face lit up. "Of course! A simple binary switch! So the robots would define right as wrong . . . "

"And wrong as right!" Carmen finished the thought.

"But it's not that easy to reprogram," Floop said, frowning.

"Well, figure it out!" Carmen told him. "Meanwhile, we'll try to stop the Spy Kids from leaving the castle."

"I'll try," Floop said. "But—"

Carmen wasn't listening. She was leading the rest of her family down another secret hallway, toward the Grand Room, where Lisp was waiting.

The four of them burst into the room, ready for anything. Almost.

"Yikes!" Juni cried when he saw who else was waiting for them.

Minion stood in the center of the room. His transformation into the most hideous Fooglie ever was complete. Now he had four heads—and four hands. A strange arm stuck out from the back of his neck.

Next to Minion stood Ms. Gradenko, with most of her hair burned off.

"Minion! What happened to you?" Mr. Lisp gasped. He looked horrified at the sight of the disgusting Fooglie.

"Don't worry, I think it's reversible," Minion replied. "I think."

"Fine. Whatever," Mr. Lisp said. "As long as you can deliver my army. Is it ready?"

"You aren't going anywhere," Mr. Cortez interrupted. "Not with those robots, at least."

"That's what *you* think," Mr. Lisp said. He nodded toward the secret agents who had arrived with Ms. Gradenko.

Instantly, Mr. and Mrs. Cortez sprang into action. They were still the world's best spies, and they knew it. They spun around, ready to fight all four of their opponents.

But first . . .

"Juni! Carmen! Close your eyes!" Mr. Cortez

called. "We don't want you to see this!"

Juni and Carmen obeyed. They squeezed their eyes shut tight. But they didn't close their ears. They could hear their parents smacking the agents, one after the other.

When the kids opened their eyes a few moments later, all four agents were lying at their mom's and dad's feet. They had been knocked out cold.

"Awesome!" Juni cried.

"Excellent!" Carmen said.

Just then the two huge doors behind them burst open. The full army of Spy Kids—all five hundred—stood ready to fight!

"Whoa!" Carmen muttered. "That's a lot of robots!"

"Okay," her dad said after a moment. "Here's what we do. I'll take the hundred on the right. Your mother will take the hundred on the left. Carmen, you take the hundred center left. Juni, take the hundred center right. . . ."

Good plan, Carmen thought. But are you *kidding*? Are we really supposed to fight a hundred powerful robots—each?

She checked out her dad's face.

Yes. He was definitely serious.

Wow, Carmen thought. He has a lot of faith in us!

The robots marched toward them, ready to strike.

"Wait, Dad. That only adds up to four hundred,"

Juni said suddenly. "And there's five hundred robots total. We need one more person!"

He's right, Carmen realized. Again. But who was going to help them now?

CHAPTERTWENTY-FIVE

The robots continued to approach the Cortez family. Suddenly, a stained glass window behind them broke—and a man swung into the castle on a long cable.

"Uncle Machete!" Juni and Carmen cried in unison.

"Hello, little brother," Machete greeted their dad.

Machete shot all of them a quick smile. Then he got into a karate position, ready for anything.

Mr. Lisp called out to the robot army. "Children! Tear them apart limb by limb!"

The robots marched forward in a huge mass. Carmen and Juni jumped out of the way.

I'm tough, Carmen thought. But not *that* tough!

She had no idea how to fight so many robots at once.

But the Spy Kids didn't attack the Cortezes.

They marched straight over to Mr. Lisp, Ms. Gradenko, and Minion—and began tossing them in the air, like stuffed dolls.

"All right!" Juni shouted.

Carmen gave her brother a high-five. "Floop did it!" she cried. "He changed the program in their brains!"

Floop appeared in the doorway, smiling.

Juni ran over to him. "How did you do it?" he asked his TV hero. "What did you teach the robots?"

Floop shrugged. "It's not so much what I taught them," he said, smiling down at Juni. "It's more about what *you* taught *me*. You won today, Juni— and not because you were the biggest or the strongest. You won because you were pure of heart and mind."

He reached out to shake Juni's hand.

Juni gave Floop a gigantic smile. Then he turned back to his family. His father and Uncle Machete were finally face-to-face.

"I'm glad you came back," Juni's dad said to Machete. "It's been a long time."

"Too long," Machete agreed.

"What happened to us?" Juni's dad asked. "It's been so long, I can't remember."

Machete looked embarrassed. "You know what? I can't remember either!" he admitted with a large laugh.

The two men put their arms around each other and hugged.

Then Mr. and Mrs. Cortez took their children aside.

"There's something we have to tell you," Mr. Cortez began to explain.

"Your father and I are secret agents," Mrs. Cortez went on.

"Uh, we know," Juni said.

"And there's something we have to tell *you*," Carmen spoke up.

"That's right," Juni said with a wink at his sister. "We're secret agents too!"

For a moment, their parents just stared at them. Then they smiled.

"From now on, we make all our decisions as a family," Mrs. Cortez said.

"Right," Mr. Cortez agreed.

Whatever, Carmen thought. She was just glad to *be* a family again! She didn't even mind having to hang out with Juni anymore. He wasn't so bad for a seven-year-old.

When the kids and their parents reached home the next day, they received a message from Devlin, the head of the OSS.

"Cortezes! I'm so glad you're back!" Devlin greeted them. He was speaking through a secret spy communication device in their television. "The OSS needs you! An emergency situation has come up in the Far East. I need to send you both right away."

"Sorry, Devlin," Mrs. Cortez answered. "But we haven't talked about this as a family yet."

Mr. Cortez nodded. "If Ingrid and I *do* come out of retirement, it will have to be a decision that's up to us *and* our kids."

Devlin shook his head. "No. I don't mean *you*, Gregorio. I mean Carmen and Juni. I have an assignment for *them!*"

Cool! When do we start? Carmen thought.

But Juni had another idea. "Devlin, if you want the Cortezes, you take *all* the Cortezes," he said.

"Yeah," Carmen agreed, giving their mom and dad a hug. "From now on, whatever we do, we do together. Spy work is easy. But keeping a family together is a lot harder. And *that's* a mission worth fighting for!"